Blood & Butlers

S.J. Frey

DEDICATION

I would like to take a moment to thank my friends and family for supporting me through this journey of my literary career. You have all been there for me since the beginning, and I don't think I could have reached my goal without any of you.

I want to dedicate my first novel to the love of my life Nathaniel. Words can't describe the amount of love and support you've given me throughout this process, and I wouldn't be where I am without you. Thank you.

CONTENTS

DISCLAIMER

Book Cover Design by: betibup33design
Author Photography by: Naomi Hoover
Author Photo Editing by: Monique Layzell Art Prints

ONE

"Okay, Mom, try not to raise too much hell."

Slowly I let my hand graze the top of the marble slab that held my mother's name. It's only been a short three months since her passing, but it feels like it was yesterday. A few times, I would come to the grave and talk to her. To think a simple cold could take out an active person like my mother. Then again, it wasn't just a cold, was it? Mom was sick for a while and never said a thing. She was too stubborn and didn't want anyone to worry about her.

The sky is starting to turn grey as the air shifts slightly, running small chills down my back. I have every right to be in a cemetery. I hate the feeling I get walking through the tombstones. It's as if something will rip through the ground and grab my ankles.

I fight the urge to run and slowly make my way back to the beat-up station wagon that sits on the gravel

1

road. The blue color and wood panel stick out like a sore thumb against the darkening sky. The door creaks open as I pull it as far as it could go and slid my body onto the cracking leather seats. Just as I shut the door, the rain began to pelt my cracked windshield. Sighing, I sit there for a moment to wait for some of the showers to pass over before I go to the main road. The last thing I needed is to hydroplane because of my tires.

My poor station wagon is on its last leg. The windshield cracked from a rock that bounced off a truck, and the floor was so rusted that, with enough force, I could probably push my feet through and Flintstone my way around. Then there is the brown leather interior that is breaking apart. I think I went through two spools of duct tape patching the beast back together. Throughout all its imperfections, the thing still runs and gets me from point A to point B.

My eyes shift to my mother's grave once more. I watch the rain come to a stop as I recall the whole reason I wanted this wagon in the first place. This wagon is my first car. My mom promised to match whatever I saved during the summer of my Junior year in high school. I picked this wagon because it reminded me so much of her.

Mom used to tell me stories from when she was my age. She grew up in the 70s and was a bit of a wild child. For some reason, this wagon reminded me of the younger version of my mother in her stories.

I smile at her grave and then look at my reflection in the window. There are bags under my eyes, and my hair is a mess. I can't remember the last time I brushed it. The long drive from New York to Virginia was tiring from the get-go, and staying in a crappy motel didn't help my insomnia either.

After everything with the house is complete, I have plans on going back to New York and never looking back. There was nothing left in Virginia for me anymore, so why return?

I turn the key and let the engine warm-up slightly before carefully applying pressure to the gas. I skillfully pull around the stone path of the cemetery and onto the main road. If I didn't get to the house in time, I knew that my Aunt Kat was going to have a fit.

The house still looks the same, the shutters are hanging off the hinges of the first-floor windows, and the walkway is still slightly overgrown with weeds. Mom and I didn't have any idea on how to fix the shutters, and the plants just took over. As I pull up to the house, I recognize Aunt Kat's green Kia in the driveway. I can only imagine how long she was waiting for me.

The moment I walk into the door, I am nearly trampled on by a tall woman with curly red hair. I am being squeezed to death and couldn't get a word out as the squeezing became tighter. Aunt Kat notices my struggle and instantly let me go. Aunt Kat wasn't my real aunt, she was a childhood friend of my mothers, and I rarely saw her. She only came to see me more in the final weeks.

"Sorry, Liz. I got a little carried away there. It's just-

- it's been so long since I last saw you."

"It's alright, Aunt Kat," I smile.

The once lively home is now a stark reminder of how things used to be. I am half expecting Mom to come around the corner with a smile on her face, but I knew it wouldn't happen. The house is empty.

All the furniture is gone. The creepy figurines my mother collected now call home to an old lady down the street, and all our family pictures are sitting in a box by the front door. It's hard to believe that all my childhood memories are now in a box.

"Alright, let's get the attic cleared out before the realtor comes."

Aunt Kat's voice seems to pull me away from my trance and slowly brings me back down to the tormented reality that I now live. She is right. If we didn't clear out before the realtor came, then we might not close on the home.

Slowly I follow Aunt Kat up the steps to the second floor, and I stop a few feet in front of Mom's room and frown. The door is open, and everything is gone. Her bed, clothes, perfume, everything that was my mother is now gone. I can feel tears prick the corners of my eyes and had to keep walking towards the task at hand. I can't let my emotions get the best of me now; I had a job to do.

Walking up to Aunt Kat, I watch her pull the little string that is attached to a trap door in the ceiling. The ladder came shooting down, making me jump slightly as the clattering sound echoed throughout the empty house.

"I was able to get rid of some decorations your mom had along with some clothing and furniture. There are still a few boxes that need to be sorted through," She says as she climbs up to the attic's opening.

I was thankful for Aunt Kat. I wouldn't be able to get all the preparation done or selling the house on my own without her.

Entering the attic, I greet the musty smell of mothballs that littered the ground. Mom must have done that to make sure the mice didn't get into the boxes. Quietly I sit on the ground and start to go through a box filled with papers. Most of it is old bills and coupons. It was junk, in my opinion. Sighing, I grab the box and sift through some more papers before I deemed it was trash. Pushing that box aside, I grab another one.

"Oh, look at this," Aunt Kat coos.

Looking up, I smile, seeing her holding a onesie that belonged to me when I was a baby. I roll my eyes and snatch it out of her hand to throw onto the trash pile. There is no reason to hold onto things like that anymore.

Aunt Kat gave a face and started to go through another box that held some papers and other documents. Most of them are old medical bills that my mother had been hiding from me. She pulled some papers out and gave them a once over before placing them onto the trash pile.

"So, any luck with any guys at school?" She asks as she wiggles her eyebrows.

I gave her a look and crossed my arms over my chest. Picking up a piece of old newspaper, I wadded it up into a paper ball at threw it at her. The older woman ducks while laughing and then reaches behind her to grab it and throw it right back at me. I caught it with one hand and sigh.

"Not a chance. I don't have time for guys besides, none of them want a serious girl, they want a girl they can sleep with on the first night."

Since I recently graduated, trying to find a new job in my career is going to be hard. I didn't have time to be worrying about guys. It wasn't like being with a guy is going to be beneficial to me in the long run. Just look at my mother; she was left pregnant by my father without another word of where he was going, and after twenty years, I never received a phone call from the man. If there were men like that in this world, then it was better off to be alone.

Aunt Kat only exhales loudly. "You will find someone someday, Lizzy. When you least expect it."

I didn't want to talk about the subject anymore. We need to get this attic cleaned out before the realtor arrives. The realtor was a real hassle to deal with in the beginning, and I would rather not be around when she comes by again. I never met a woman that could smile to your face and yet be so stuck up at the same time. New York City is full of people like her, but most of them keep to themselves. This woman, Cathy, was nosey and wanted nothing more than her commission.

After what seemed like forever, we clean up the first round of boxes. Going back up, we began the second round. Sifting through, I find more old bills, pictures, silly awards I won in grade school and a soccer trophy for that one time I tried to play soccer, failed, and quit. I might keep the cup, though. I push through to the bottom of the box, and I find a thick, yellow folder with the string broken. There are water stains covered in little black spots that scream mold. It was sitting at the very bottom so naturally it would get ruined; this attic leaked all the time.

I slip my hand through the flap and pull out a thick stack of papers. They are so stained that it is hard to make heads or tails of what is on the paper. The only thing I could make out from the envelope is my name and certain words from the packet itself.

"Hey, Aunt Kat? What do you make of this?" I ask, holding the papers out to her.

Aunt Kat pulls her reading glasses from her back pocket and presses them to her face. She peers closely at the brittle pages as she tries to read what I couldn't. If her face were any closer to the paper, she would be kissing it.

"I can't tell you what it is. A will? Maybe?" she says, flipping through some of the other pages. Some of them start to rip in her hands as she turns them over.

A will? It couldn't be Mom's; I already had her paperwork from when she passed. Was this a backup copy?

"Here!" She exclaims, pointing to a page towards the end of the packet.

"It says here. 'The final testament of Edmund J. Montgomery, written and curated by The Law Offices of William Galloway & Co.' Why does that name sound familiar?" She stops and looks up at me. "Lizzy, I think this is your father's."

It feels like someone took a rock and jammed it down my throat, only to push it into my stomach. My heart is beating rapidly, and I have no clue why. I never met my father, so why did I feel as if he would walk up right behind me at this moment? This document is proof that he is just as gone now as he was back then. Why would he send a will to a child whom he has never seen? More importantly, why would my mother keep it and not tell me? I couldn't tell what hurt most, the deception, or the discovery.

Aunt Kat sensed my distracted state and cleared her throat.

"I can't tell what everything entails; the papers are beaten up. The only thing I can make out is that it was sent out about four years ago, other than that, it's in ruins."

So, for four years, while I was in school, Mom held onto the most significant piece of information about my life and failed to share it with me? Well, she kept her sickness a secret. I shouldn't be too surprised.

"Where is the office?" I ask, looking at the paper.

Aunt Kat points to the smudged letter that read a somewhat legible address. The office is in town, which meant my father must have lived in the same area. So, for twenty years, no phone call, no letter, no visit and he lived so close, but dared to give me his stuff when he died? I have half a mind to just chuck the papers and move on with my life, but there is something inside my heart that wanted to know more about him. He has been a mystery in my life, and I feel like this will is a step closer to finally solving it. I came to terms with my mother's passing, and now I need to come to terms with my father's disappearance.

"Look sugar. I wouldn't worry about it too much. Just go to the lawyer and see what they say." Aunt Kat smiles.

"You're right. We should get this trash out of here before Cathy comes," I say as I quickly gather up as many bags as I can and shove the packet of papers into my armpit.

When we put the trash is on the curb, I left the key in the secured pack on the door. The house is no longer my childhood home, my safe sanctuary, my mother's heart, and her soul. It is now just a house. Aunt Kat hugs me tightly and begs me to visit her from time to time. Of course, I counter with her visiting my best friend and me in the big city. I watch her get into her green Kia and slowly drove down the street, around the corner and out of sight until the next time I saw her. When will that be? I have no idea.

The wind is starting to pick up again as the

threatening smell of fresh rain began to rise from the earth. At any moment, it will storm, and I need to find a place to stay for the night. I promised Amy I would wait for her before getting a better hotel, but she didn't arrive in town yet. So, the run-down motel will have to do until she gets back to me.

Just as I get into my car, I watch as a blue minivan pulls into the driveway and the realtor's car arriving right after it. That is my cue to leave. I can't sit and watch their happy faces as they tour through their new home. I put my car into gear and pull away from the curb. I didn't care where I am going, but at that moment, I knew I have to get away from here.

.

TWO

I don't think I will get over the shock of knowing my mother kept something from me all these years. First, it was my father's will, and then it was her sickness. What was next? A rich Grandmother I never thought I had?

Still, it is hard to know that the only person you have in your life kept something so monumental away from you. She left me behind with too many questions like: Why would she keep me from this? Was she trying to protect me? a

The yellowed envelope crinkles in my hand as I pull out the packet of moldy papers. Most of the ink washed away from our leaky roof. I can barely make out any of the words except the letterhead that is still intact.

"Law Offices of William Galloway & Co. 2325 Main Street, Johnstown VA"

Well, at least I knew where to go. I scrunch my face up to the paper to try and make out the rest of it, but my dim car light didn't help. The documents are so fragile they are falling apart in my hands. People are staring at me as they walk to their cars from the burger joint I stopped by. I huff, throwing my head back and let the papers fall to my lap while the raindrops dot my windshield.

Sighing, I carefully stuff the papers back into the envelope and grab my phone.

Amy texted me a bunch of times, and I could tell she was getting restless.

A: Hey! I finally got my project in! Are we still on for tonight?

Crap. I forgot for a brief second that Amy was driving from New York to stay with me. I also forgot to tell her that the house is no more and that I didn't have the hotel room to stay in yet. I've been wasting time.

A: Are you there?

A: GPS says I'm only six hours away!

A: Hope you're okay. I am stopping by a rest stop. Call me if you need me.

I want to kick myself for not texting her back right away. Amy is always a bit of a worrywart. Ever since we became friends and roommates, she still did the best to look out for me, even when I was going through the law for months of my mother's death. She is the sister I never had. If it wasn't for being there for me when things went sour, I'm not sure how I would have survived.

I am looking at the last text message I quickly type up a reply.

Me: Hey! Sorry for not responding. I got caught up

with Aunt Kat at the house.

A: It's okay! I was getting a little worried about you. Glad to hear everything went well.

Me: Of course, you were worried, you always are! You'll never guess what I found.

A: What?

Me: A will from my father

There is a slight pause, and I instantly feel guilty thinking she might have been pulled over for texting and driving. Or maybe she is in shock like I was. Before I can type, my phone chimed.

A: Oh, wow! What did it say? Sorry, GPS took me to a U-turn. I'm about four hours out.

Me: No worries. I can hardly read it. It's falling apart. I'm on my way to see the lawyer about it. The sooner I get it done, the better. I'll tell you more when you get into town. Text me when you arrive.

A: Okay! Make sure you get all the details!

Me: Okay. Drive safe.

When Amy didn't text me back, I shove the phone back into my bag and start up my car. The wagon roars to life, and I slowly back out from my parking spot.

The rain shifted into nothing more than a light mist as I drive through town. Main Street is always busy with all the different shops and restaurants. Most of the places Mom and I went to are still around while others closed due to the economy. This area doesn't get many tourists, so jobs are scarce, and the income isn't there.

With so little to offer, it was one of the driving reasons why I wanted to make something of myself and give mom a better life. New York City is extensive, with many jobs, shopping, and homes. If I land even a semi-good job with my photography skills, we would be all set. Johnstown looked like a dreary ghost town when I left. I turn onto the main strip, and I can see nothing changed.

The row homes of small businesses still line the right side of the street, while restaurants and retail shops lined the left side. If I drove a few hundred feet more, I would hit the highway and see the mall. Behind all the shops sat old colonel homes and the old town hall. It is a quiet place and peaceful during the day, but at night everyone came out of the dark holes they were hiding in.

Mom used to tell me stories of people in the ER with broken faces because of bar fights in town. Out of the corner of my eye, I notice a new building that wasn't there the last time I came to town. It is a night club painted black with lime green trim. A large neon sign flashed "Viper," and a giant green cartoon snake grinned on the one side of the building. It looks cheesy, but maybe it would be something fun that Amy would like to do later.

Double-checking the address, I slow down when I got closer. I find the first parking spot I could on the street and carefully parallel parked. For a split second, I am worried my old wagon won't fit between the Volkswagen bug and Mustang, but I manage to make it work.

The air feels colder, and I quickly rush down the

street. The royal blue sign with gold letters sticks out like a sore thumb, reading "Galloway & Co."

In a way, I am nervous to see what was in store. I can't make out the words on the paper and hope the law office would be able to help. These moldy papers are the first thing I ever received from the man who left everything behind.

Am I still angry? Yes. Do I want to rip this will up to shreds? Hell yes! Was there a part of me that had a glimmer of hope? Maybe. As much as I hate that man, I have questions. I knew most of them wouldn't have answers, but anything was better than nothing.

Walking up to the steps, I look through the large front window to see the waiting area is empty. When I open the door, the warm scent of vanilla hit my face as I opened the door. It is soothing and makes me relax a little as the chime above my head silences when the door shut behind me.

A woman is sitting behind a window in the wall and look to be typing away. On closer inspection, she is playing solitaire to pass the time. I clear my throat as gently as I could, so I don't startle her.

"Excuse me?" I timidly ask.

The woman turns around in her chair. She pushes up her glasses, with chains dangling from the arms of her glasses. She reminds me of a little old librarian. The name tag shines brightly, with Delores engraved into the gold plate. Her gray hair is pulled back into a braid, and her old paisley sweater blinds me with colors of burnt orange and brown. She certainly looks like a

Delores.

"Yes, dear, what can I help you with?" She smiles.

"I found this envelope addressed to me from my father, and it's damaged. I was hoping someone could help me?"

Gently she takes the moldy papers from my hand and looks them over — her face twists in disgust at the quality and maybe from the musty smell.

"Yes, I see. I will let Mr. Galloway know you are here, and he will be right with you. He is currently on a call," she says as she writes something down on a yellow sticky note and gets up from her seat.

I watch her walk away and wonder just what my father left behind. A small part of me hopes it wasn't going to give me more of a headache. After waiting for a little at the window, I felt silly standing and decided to sit down. The cushions on the white leather couch squeak slightly under my weight. I wonder how many people came to this building. A lot of things changed since I left for school. I only came home for Christmas but never went into the town. If everything keeps changing, I soon won't recognize this town in ten years.

"Elizabeth, thank you for stopping by," a male voice says, catching me off guard. The man grins and extends a hand for me to shake.

I immediately stand up and extend my hand to reach his. He has a firm grip to which I tried to match, but my fingers ache under pressure. He must have sensed my pain and instantly let go.

"Sorry, I tend to get carried away," he grins some more.

"It's alright. Really."

"Why don't you follow me to my office? We have a lot to discuss."

The man gently places his hand on the small of my back and guides me through the door. The door leads down a hallway with four other entries. The first door on the left is for Delores. I can tell because I can see her peeking through the crack in the doorway as we walk by her. The other two doors are labeled for bathrooms while the last door at the end of the hallway has a shiny black plaque with gold lettering reading "William Galloway." The closer we walk towards his office, the more nervous I became.

He opens the door for me, and I am greeted with the soft scent of more vanilla and lavender thanks to the air freshener on the wall. Instantly I start to relax as my eyes wandered around the room. There are books along the windowsill with various awards and degrees on the wall. A long brown couch sits against one wall, and a large oak desk with two wooden chairs are across the room.

William closes the door behind us and points to one of the wooden chairs.

"Please have a seat."

I nod and gently lower myself into a seat while he sits in the black leather chair on the opposite side of me. I watch as he reaches down to grab something and hear keys jingling before a drawer opening. He grabs a manila folder and places it on the desk between us.

My eyes wander over the folder and to the moldy stack of papers I brought in. I wonder if Mr. Galloway might have a copy or something. Maybe I can finally get this stressful day over with, so I can get some rest.

"Elizabeth Evans," he says softly, running a hand through his slicked-back hair. "I'm sorry to hear about your mother." His eyes meet mine, and I instantly squirm in my seat.

Talking about my mother's death is something I try to avoid.

"It's fine, thank you. And please call me Lizzy. Elizabeth is too old fashion," I smile.

William smiles too and seems to relax now that the awkward moment is over. "Yes, very well, Izzy. Let's see here."

Carefully he pulls a stack of neat, white paper from the folder and starts to go through them.

"Okay. It says here 'upon my death, all of my possessions will go to my one and only child, Elizabeth Marie Evans.' It looks like your father left you his manor on Willowbrook Drive. It seems he did not specify any other possessions." He states and looks up from the papers to my stunned face.

Did he say manor? Like, as in a mansion?! What kind of man has an estate in Johnstown, Virginia? I am heavily questioning my father and wonder what my mother was thinking. This man had to be a mob boss or something because I know for a fact that mansions aren't something people can afford around here.

William took a moment to let me recover before I can speak.

"A manor? Well, that's very generous from a man who walked out."

Now my anger is starting to return, remembering how much I despise him for leaving my mother and me. Then to top everything, he left me a manor, which I could have sold years ago to pay for the treatment my mother needed to get better. Then again, Mom was the one who hid the will, and her sickness wasn't something either of us predicted. I am pretty sure I'm just trying to find reasons to be angry now, instead of reasoning.

I take a big breath and count to ten before speaking once more. "Can you sell the thing? I do not want to live in a manor, or in Johnstown for that matter."

William looks a little disappointed when he should be kissing my feet. Lawyers love liquidations and making commissions. Instead, he places the stack of paperwork into the folder, along with my moldy paper, and hands it to me.

"Unfortunately, it's much more than just a manor. It gave exclusive instructions that you now own the manor and everything inside. It means there are valuables within the premises that you would need to go through," William says with a smile.

Why do I feeling like he is enjoying this?

"Look, I just went through all of this with my mother's passing, and I honestly don't have the energy to go through this again. Let alone trying to pack up, sort out, and sell a manor."

I'm not lying. I am emotionally and physically exhausted. There is nothing more I want to do than to find a motel, take a hot bath, wait for Amy, and go to bed.

William nods and sits back in his chair. "I would offer my help, but this is a two-person office. I'm needed 24/7."

This whole situation is starting to irritate me more. Maybe I will sleep in the overly sized manor instead of a crappy motel room depending on how dirty and dusty the mansion is, of course. However, no matter what choice I make, there's a good chance I might get bedbugs. Great.

"You remind me so much of your father. The way you stare intently at the floor when lost in thought or daydreaming."

I feel my cheeks burn a little as I push some of my long hair out of my face. "You knew my father?" I ask.

William nods, "I grew up with him. It was only natural that he made me draft his will when I became a lawyer.

Now my curiosity has the best of me. What else did William know about my father? Like, was my old man a drug dealer or something that he could afford a manor in this town?

"What else can you tell me about him?" I question.

"Well, let's see. Your father was a smart man; he graduated top of our class, and he was very successful in D.C. Edmund had a way with words and was one hell of a congressman." William smiles with pride as he looks out the window.

I am trying to picture why my mother would be into a man involved in politics. She was a free spirit like me, expressive and caring. Most people in politics looked like they all had wooden sticks up their butts.

William hands me a picture frame with two smiling men in front of a large building that looked like an old church or school.

"That was your father and me at Cambridge. He was a dreamer that one. He wanted to make the world a better place."

My eyes scan the picture before looking up at William. He looks almost the same except for a little grey in his hair and the 70s suit that was missing. My eyes then wander to my father. He was handsome, with dark hair and soft brown eyes. I could see why Mom fell in love with him. It almost makes me feel sad for not meeting him at least once. Almost.

"Thank you for showing me," I nod and hand back the photo. William takes back the picture and places it with the other images.

This situation is starting to get more awkward as I stood up, wanting to flee. I am trying to hold onto the feeling of not liking my father desperately. Still, I could feel my walls slowly start to dissolve.

William smiles and hands me the folder with a sticky note attached to it. "Look at the manor and see what you want to do with it. Call me with any questions."

I stare at the pale-yellow sticky note with an address

and phone number neatly written in cursive. "Thanks, I appreciate all of your help," I nod as I hold the folder to my chest. Slowly William places a silver key on the desk and slides it towards me. Silently I pick it up and shove it in my pocket.

"That key should open the front door. If you have any problems, please call me." William says as if he had no care in the world. I, on the other hand, couldn't match his smile.

Without another word, I turn and walk down the hallway and out onto the wet streets. The moment I slam my car door shut, I try to process what just happened. I take a few deep breaths before closing my eyes and lean my head back on the headrest.

What the hell just happened? The only thing I was expecting out of all of this was maybe a clock or something random that could be left behind. Not a manor! It is taking everything in me not to pinch myself to see if I am dreaming. Now it is up to me to figure out what I wanted to do with it.

The little sticky note is calling me as I stare at it from the driver's seat. I pick it up and play with it between my fingers for a moment. I am tired and want to shower. I smell like musty clothes and sweat.

"2396 Willow Brook Drive," I sigh.

With my luck, the manor could be in bad shape and would have to be torn down. I tap the sticky note against the steering wheel in thought. I could always ignore the manor and let it rot, but that would lead to more problems.

Why not? I do have three hours to kill after all. I turn on the car and start my way down the street. Getting onto the highway, I make a right turn and drive towards 2396 Willow Brook Drive, trying hard not to regret my decision. here.

THREE

I'm not sure what I will be expecting. This place could be a complete crap-hole, and I would have to demolish it.

As I round the bend, it leads to another road. I stare down the row of trees as my path reaches a hidden dirt road up a slight slope. The trees line up the road heading up the side of a mountain, guiding my way to the manor. At least I hope this is taking me to the estate. I am so far away from the town that I start to lose my cell service.

"Great." I groan.

My service completely drops, and I lose internet connection. My anxiety began to spike as I drive further into the unknown, wondering if this is the correct way or not. I knew it is, but I want the safety blanket of my phone by my side to guide my way. Anything can happen. After sitting and stalling, I drive down the single dirt road, letting my mind go numb with uncertainty.

"This is a bad idea," I keep whispering to myself the further I drive.

It was too late now. It isn't like I could turn around. This road is a one-car road! As I came around another curve, the trees start to part to reveal an opening. The moment I clear the trees, I'm in shock. The dirt path leads to a circular driveway with a stone fountain in the middle. The big building that sits behind the fountain makes me grow pale. It's at least two floors since the building is two windows high and eight windows long. The stairs leading up to the dark, double oak doors are slate grey that contrasted with the white columns that held the porch balcony above them. At the top of the stone stairs sits two white angel statues on opposite sides. I swear I'm looking at some Greek museum or even the Taj Mahal from how tidy it looks. No dirt or vines are growing on the statues or the stone porch. It was almost too clean. Why do I get the sense that someone was still living here?

Slowly, I stop my car in front of the stairs and kill the engine. This place makes me look like a peasant in comparison. I might need to put a formal gown on before walking in. I begrudgingly get out of my car and stare at the massive building before me. My feet begin to drag towards the stone stairs, and I nearly trip myself. My palms start to sweat as my fight or flight instinct begins to take over.

What was I so scared? Oh, maybe I'm intruding on

some squatters that live here, and they will murder me and put me in their chili!

No. I highly doubt that that would happen.

I grab the brass door knocker and slam it three times. Taking a step back and I wait nervously. There is a clicking noise from the other end, making me jump slightly. So, people are living here! But who?

The door opens a crack. It's dark inside, and I can't see who opened it. I decide to be brave and take a step closer.

"H-Hello?" I call out.

Nothing.

"My name is Elizabeth Evans? My father owned this manor and entrusted it to me when he died." Reaching into my bag, I pull out the crumpled stack of papers from the old will, totally forgetting I left the right copy in the car.

The door opens a little more, and a gloved hand reaches out, snatches the papers from me, and then slams the door in my face. It all happened so fast I wasn't sure what is going on.

"H-Hey!" I yell, slamming my fist on the door. I am tired and hungry and didn't want to deal with this right now.

"I don't know who you are, but this not how you treat a lady! Hello!?!"

As my fist left the door, it opens inward once more. This time the door opens all the way and a tall man stands before me. He has short black hair and the brightest blue eyes I have ever seen. They remind me of a pool, so crystal clear that I want to jump in and disturb the still water. He's wearing a black suit with a black tie. It's a little strange, considering outfits like that didn't belong in a town like this. He must have been amused by my gawking because his lips quirk up into a half smug smile.

I break out of my trance and stare at him, hand on my hip, trying to assert my dominance even though he is much taller than I am.

"It's incredibly rude to slam the door on someone," I state.

He looks at me and reaches into his blazer to grab my papers to hand back to me.

"I do apologize madam, but you have to understand. We get a lot of people wanting to buy this manor or claim that they are the rightful owner. You'll have to excuse my ignorance."

Okay. Now, this is getting weirder. Not only does this stranger have an accent, but who the hell talks so proper? Who is he? A Downtown Abbey extra?

"It's alright, I guess. The real question is, who and why are you here? I was under the impression that this place is empty." I ask, feeling a little nervous.

A small smile crosses his face as he gave a little bow at the waist.

"I am Darren Chambers, butler and current caretaker of the Montgomery Manor."

Oh-kay. Not sure what century Darren is from, but he needs a reality check.

He stood up straight and moved a little to the side

to give me room to walk by him.

"We were wondering when the new heir would arrive," he says, as I slowly make my way past the threshold.

The foyer is elaborate. The floors shine with a delicate design, the polished marble and a grand staircase leading to the second floor splits at the top with hallways to the left and right. Each inch of the wall is in a deep red wallpaper with a gold design peeking through the massive amounts of art and pictures.

I immediately groaned. There are so many things from what I could see. I can only imagine the work I have to do to clean everything out. The place is so vast, and it is going to take more than a weekend to get everything packed and moved to sell.

Hearing the click from the door behind me, I jump. I look at Darren, who ignores my surprised look and starts to walk away.

"Follow me, Miss Elizabeth, and I can show you to your room."

Right away, I don't like this. I wasn't planning on staying or keeping the manor. Not to mention, I didn't have the money to pay for the utilities or the staff. At the moment, it looks like it is only Darren.

I stop following him at the foot of the stairs and shake my head. "I am sorry, but I don't plan on living here. I didn't know who my father was or that he left me a mansion. I'm sorry, but I don't think I'm going to keep the manor. I don't have the means to pay you." I say carefully, even though I felt terrible. This manor is probably his home, and I am destroying it for him.

Darren turns to look at me and sighs in annoyance, but he smiles anyway. "Do what you want. This manor is yours. Your father left it to you. So, you can do whatever you wish."

I shake my head a little and look down at my feet. I notice my shoes are dirty from the dust and worn out from the constant moving; I look like a bum. Maybe that's why Darren shut the door on me at first. Besides, I want to find a place to stay before the night gets darker, this forest is a maze, and I didn't feel like getting lost.

Darren only stands there staring at me, making me feel more uncomfortable. "If you leave, you will be more tired than you already are. And by the looks of it, you could also use a bath," he smirks.

I'm not sure if he is trying to be funny or if he didn't know what he is saying. Either way, I feel insulted. I purse my lips and turn right around to walk away.

"Right, I'll see you later," I say, waving my hand, walking towards the door. I am too tired to argue with someone right now.

My eyes are glued to the ground as my brain bounces around to come up with a game plan. I'm still waiting for Amy to message me once she gets into town, only then can I figure out where we would stay. In the meantime, I am limited to what I can afford. I wouldn't mind sleeping in my car, but water tends to leak through the window seals. In an instant, I bump into something and look up to see Darren standing right in front of me. I blink and glance back at the staircase before back at him. We are standing halfway to the door. How the hell did he get to me so fast? Then again, he did have long legs; he probably only had to take three steps.

"Sorry, I didn't know you were going to jump out at me," I frown.

"It's alright. Why don't you stay here? You own this place now. It would make more sense to stay here than a hotel. Plus, I can cook dinner. It would be nice to break out the fine china again." He says with another smile.

The guilt starts to creep up again. Darren is probably here alone since my father died. The way he is acting, it's hard to tell if he wants me to stay or leave. Maybe I'm thinking about it all wrong.

The fatigue is setting into my bones, and I still need a shower. Plus, if I didn't go to a motel, I can save the money for when I travel back to New York. My growling stomach makes the final decision, and I swallow hard to try and not let my stomach embarrass me further.

"Okay, I guess I could stay." I feel like a broken, battered woman accepting to stay here.

"Follow me." He grins and gently grabs my elbow. His hands are cold to the touch but slowly warm up. I didn't mind it, but the moment his fingertips reaches the same temperature as my skin, he let go.

I follow behind him up the stairs, turning to walk

down the left hallway. I keep quiet and stare at all the pictures and art that scatter the walls. Whoever my father was, he loved art. A new fact that only deepened the mystery of who my father was. When I was young, I used to ask my mom about him, who he was, more importantly, where he was. However, no matter how many times I asked, she always got depressed and didn't say anything.

Looking at Darren's broad back, I clear my throat to get his attention as we walk. "Darren, was it? How much do you know of my father?" I ask.

Darren stays quiet for a moment and comes to a halt in front of a dark wooden door. He turns to look at me and appears to be even more annoyed than before. His face softens a little, and his eyes glide towards the window.

"Your father was a good man. He worked hard and gave us a place to stay. He loved your mother and you dearly. He used to talk about you two all the time, even up until his passing."

I feel weird. I should feel sorry, but instead, I stand there, awkwardly. I didn't know much about my father up until today. Now I have all of this information coming at me. I don't want to talk about my father anymore with him. My stomach is churning, and I need to stop before I get sick.

"You say us, who else lives here?" I question. I hope there wasn't a whole army of servants that I had to lay off inevitably.

Darren raises an eyebrow. "Yes, there are two more

servants that worked under your father. There is Reginald, who maintains the gardens, library, and east downstairs corridors. And then there is Amaryllis, who tends to the western upstairs corridor, carport, and ballroom. I, of course, handle everything else." He smiles with a sense of pride.

"Wow. This place is so big it must be a tough job. Will I meet the rest of the staff?"

As much as it pains me to tell them I am going to be selling the manor, I am still slightly curious about meeting these people. Maybe I should sign the estate over to one of them. My father gave them a place to stay, so now they can own it. No hassle, right?

Darren chuckles, "You will meet Reginald, and let's hope you eventually don't meet Amarylis. She can be a troublemaker."

I nod and tuck some hair behind my ear. It's still hard to believe that a father would leave a manor like this to me. With all the furniture, art, and now employees, it was all too much for me. William did say I owned everything inside, and he wasn't kidding. The thought of going through and separating everything is starting to give me a headache.

"Well, this is your room. Your bathroom is the door on the left when you walk in. There are fresh towels and sheets for you. I will be downstairs preparing dinner. If you need anything, don't be afraid to ask." He gives another little bow and walks away towards the same way we came.

I watch for a while and yawn, opening the door to

my room. The moment I did, I am completely in shock. There is a large canopy bed in the middle of the room with dark blue bedding. The pillows are a cream color satin, and the canopy is white lace. The bed is big enough for at least three people.

Slowly, I shut the door behind me and walk over to the bed, placing a hand down on the mattress to test the firmness. I explore the room a little and run my hand over the glossy black wardrobe and vanity. This room was made for a princess, no doubt. My father must have been a damn good politician to be able to afford such luxury.

There is a door off to the right of the room that caught my attention. When I open the door, it reveals a walk-in closet with all kinds of clothes and dresses ranging in sizes. Shoes line the floor to the back of the closet. I need to take six giant-size steps to walk through it. It is only then that it dawns on me that I left my clothes in my car, so I'll have to grab something to get me by. I pick up a purple sweater that was loosely knit and a pair of black leggings. The shirt will be a little too big, but it would do for now.

The moment I open the bathroom door, I thought I died and went to heaven. The bathroom is something only seen in hotels. A large white tub with little jets is off to the right of the tiled floor, and a large vanity sink is to the left. The toilet is towards the back behind a half wall. Across from it, there is a glass shower door for the standing shower. There is too much going on, and I feel my head spin. I don't know what to do.

Looking back at the tub, I decided a nice hot bath was what I need. The jets would feel relaxing on my sore back from moving all the trash and heavy bags. I turn the knobs to let the tub fill with hot water while I undress.

There is a timer on the wall for the jets, begging me to turn them on. I set it for thirty minutes and smile, seeing the tub roar to life. The hot water starts to soothe my skin and relax my muscles as I ease myself lower into the water. My eyes close, and a sigh escapes my lips the deeper I sink my body. For a moment, all my stress from the day melted away, and the rushing thoughts came to a stop, drowned out by the sound of the rushing water and bubbling jets.

FOUR

The bath was just what I needed. After I towel dried my hair, I placed the damp towels on the counter. Once I put on my purple sweater, I tried to run my fingers through the wet rat's nest I had on my head since I could not locate a brush.

I have no intention of staying in my room all day. There is a lot of work to be done if I want to get back to New York in a timely fashion. I can start taking inventory now, and when Amy gets into town, she can help me sell everything.

My bare feet tiptoe down the carpeted hallway. As I walk by the windows on my left decorated in dark red velvet curtains, I stop to look through the glass to see how the backyard looks. There is a large garden with rose bushes of different colors, and a patio with some elegant, white, iron furniture. Trees protect the perimeter of the land, making everything calm and serene. For a brief moment, I'm at peace and forgot about everything around me.

After staring blankly for an eternity, I broke away from the window and continue down the hallway.

I stop towards the staircase and look down the carpeted stairs. A large chandelier hangs high in the foyer, showering the dark walls with multicolor dots. The brown banister leading down is so shiny and clean that I thought for sure Darren cleans it every day. Who knows? Maybe he did. The building is so elegant to the smallest detail; it is hard to believe that royalty didn't live here.

The manor is quiet, aside from the sounds coming from the large wooden door to the left of the staircase. Quietly, I tipped toed to the door and opened it a crack to see what was inside. I recognize Darren standing at the sink, washing something. Before I could get a good look at the kitchen, Darren decides to turn around. I quickly jump back so he wouldn't see me.

Carefully I walk back the hallway to the right of the kitchen and continue down the path. The decorated rug ended, and my feet touch the cold hardwood floors. A small shiver trickles down my spine as I walk past the open windows. The one thing I noticed the most about this place was the symmetry. Each floor had the same number of rooms as well as windows. It seems that everything is in perfect order and clean. Maybe my father liked it that way.

I am bored by the time I get to the end of the hallway. It is a dead-end and didn't loop around the building. Sighing, I turn around to go back to my room but stop seeing a door open.

"That wasn't open when I walked by," I whisper to myself.

Taking a quick look around, making sure no one was watching me, as I slowly walk over to the door and push it open. The door creaks loudly and gently bumps the wall when it makes contact.

The room is dark, and I am afraid to go in. Going into creepy places was one-way people died in horror movies! It will be just my luck if this manor is haunted just as much as how luxurious it is. I look back down the hallway towards the staircase to see if someone was coming. Then I look at the other door to my left to make sure no one is standing there.

When the coast is clear, I sneak into the doorway and touch the bare wall looking for the light switch, hoping nothing will grab my arm in the process. I feel the light switch with the tips of my fingers and flip it up. The room smells old and musty and grew stronger the further I walk in.

Bookcases cover the walls and full of books with rolled-up papers. The floor is filthy with open books, newspapers, and yellow folders like the ones William gave me. In the center of the room is a dark wooden desk with a red hue. Maybe it is made out of Cherry? Even more books and papers cover the surface of the desk.

For as clean as the rest of the manor is, this room is a disaster.

I sit down on the black leather chair behind the desk and look around me. I swivel the chair and glance at a cabinet against the wall that held drinking glasses and some bottles of brown fluid. I grimace at the liquid and rotate back to the desk. This room is too messy to ignore and needs cleaning first.

The air grew dusty as I pick up some papers to clean up the desk a little. Some are newer, while others are drastically older. Among the pile of books, there is a newspaper in a different language. Just who was my father?

When I was growing up, I always speculated who he was. Mom never really talked about him too much. When I asked, she would stare off into space and tell me he was a great guy, but she couldn't remember much. It got to the point where I stopped asking because I never got a real response from her.

I used to get so jealous of my friends growing up. When the parents had an open house or the father-daughter dances at school, I was teased for being the oddball. From then on, I decided that I didn't need a father in my life. I had mom, and that's all I needed.

A tear trickles down my face making me wake up from my daydream. Even though mom passed away a few months ago, it still felt fresh in my heart. I've been doing my best to keep everything under control. When I thought back at how alone mom was when I was younger makes me resent my father even more. My throat was growing tight, and it's getting hard to swallow as the guilt got stuck in my chest. I left mom alone when I left for school, and I wasn't around for her when she died. If my father was around, she didn't have to work so hard. Things would have been easier for her if she had the help. I thought I was helping by going to school to make something of myself, for us.

My emotions are getting out of control, and I slam my fist on the desk. When my fist makes contact with the hard surface, the top drawer pops open with a click. I quickly wipe my eyes and pull the drawer open all the way to see what is inside.

A black box decorated in silver trim stands out and catches my eye. As I pull it out, I notice how heavy it is, and I wondered what is inside. Based on the weight, I have to guess a rock or brick. To my dismay, the box is locked, and I need a key to open it. I gently place the box on the desk and start to rummage through the drawer. I hope I find the key to satisfy my curiosity. Instead, I see only a bunch of pictures and some more papers.

I pull out the pictures by the handful, and to my surprise, there were of my mother. A younger, healthier version of my mother was smiling back at me through the black and white barrier. I chuckle as I look at her long hair and those god-awful bell bottoms.

"Holy fringe top, Batman." I mock softly with a smile.

It's nice to see pictures like this of her. She didn't have many photos at home, and this proved how I always thought she was a flower child. My eyes scan the fringed top that stopped at her waist and then to the big round glasses she was wearing. She had her left hand up with a peace sign standing in front of a monument. I looked closer to see where she was. Frowning, I turn it over and see flawless handwriting that reads, "Lincoln Memorial, Summer '78". I did the math and realize she's only eighteen in this picture.

Smiling, I place the picture to the side to put it somewhere safe. I pick up a few more laughing at the clothing and hairstyles but stop at one photo. This one is in color. It was my mother dressed nicely in a navy-blue jumpsuit that fit with the 70s wavy hairstyle she was rocking. To the right of her was a man dressed sharply in a black suit. His hair was short, slicked back, and was as dark as his suit. His smile was gentle, and the way he looked at my mother, it wasn't hard to figure out that this was my father.

Seeing him is the first time that I was able to see any evidence of what my father looked like. Right away, I can see the resemblance of the genetics' he passed down to me. We share the same brown eyes and the dimples in our cheeks when we smile. In a way, it is nice to be able to put a face to the man I fantasized about for most of my life. However, seeing these photos still leaves me bitter with the events leading up to this moment.

Turning the picture over the date says, "Mayor's Ball 1978". My mom was eighteen in this photo too. It's crazy to see photos like this. At home, we only had pictures of her and myself as I grew up. There were no pictures of her like these.

I put the picture down with the others and stare at the box once more. I try to pry open the lid with my bare hands, but the lock is too secure. I grab the letter opener that is on the desk and try to carefully wedge the blade between the crease of the lid and box. However, it won't budge. Picking up the item, I close one eye and attempt to peer through the keyhole. I want to see what's in there so bad that it's starting to annoy me that I can't open it. Why did the box have to be locked in the first place?

"I brought you something miss," calls out an unexpecting voice.

I nearly jump out of my skin as Darren enters the room. The locked box tumbles from my hands and onto the pile of papers. My heart beats so hard that it's going to give me cardiac arrest.

I notice Darren is fighting to hide his smile as he places a silver tray down with a white mug filled with a dark brown liquid and a small plate of cheesecake. I pick up the cup and take a whiff. The sweet smell of coffee washes over me and relaxes my tense shoulders.

"I wasn't sure how you took your coffee, so I brought cream and sugar as well." He states as he starts to pick up the papers on the floor.

"Black is fine," I reply.

He stands back up and smiles, putting the papers on the desk in a neat pile. "That's how your father liked his coffee, as well."

It is clear to me that this amuses him, but I'm not. I immediately stop sipping my coffee and place the cup back down on the platter. This time I pick up my fork and begin to eat my cheesecake as Darren starts to speak again.

"I see you aren't fond of your father."

My eyes dart up at him and lock onto his eyes. He stares at me with such intensity, as if he is trying to figure out what I am going to say next.

"I can't be fond of someone if I don't know them," I comment.

Darren nods and puts his hands on the desk, leaning towards me as I lean back. I can practically smell the mint toothpaste he uses as he inches forward.

"No. I suppose you can't. However, some of us know people well and still aren't fond of them," he replies.

I stay silent as he continues.

"Your father was a remarkable man. He was smart, kind, and did what he could to help others. When my mother died, and my father left, your father was there to give me a home, food, and the discipline a young man needed. In return, I offered my employment. He was a good man and loved you and your mother very much."

"It must have been nice that he was able to give someone else a life that he had no responsibility for. If he loved us so much, then why did he leave?!" I snap.

Who is he for trying to make me feel guilty? My father left us, and as a slap to the face, he left a manor to say 'sorry.' No amount of money can heal the wounds I suffered from him not being there, and nothing can bring my mother back.

Darren must have sensed my frustration or seen it in my face as he stood back up and placed his hands behind his back.

"I beg your pardon, Miss Elizabeth. I don't know why he did what he did, and it was not right of me to say such things. Please forgive me."

I roll my eyes and pick up my plate with the cheesecake, shoving a huge piece in my mouth. Damn, this is good. Eating is the only way to distract myself and not ball my eyes out to a guy I just met. No to mention I'm pretty sure he isn't from this planet. He acts strangely. Then again, I never really had a butler before. Did they all work like this?

I realize snapping at Darren isn't the best way to release my stress. It isn't his fault, and he is kind enough to bring me cheesecake. Which, coincidentally, is my favorite.

"It's fine. Don't worry about it. I'm sorry for being rude to you." I apologize and grab my coffee to take a sip.

Darren relaxes a little and smiles again. "It's quite alright."

I gaze at him, wondering just where he came from exactly. It's obvious, from his accent, that he isn't from around here and his manors are way too proper. It's like he is from an old-timey movie or something.

"I have to run to the store for some last-minute things for dinner. Is there anything you need?" He asks, breaking my train of thought.

I think for a moment and decide there isn't, but I need to get some fresh air. Being in this stuff room is enough to make me sick. "No, but why don't I go with you? I could use some fresh air, and I can help you carry bags in," I say, standing up.

He seems surprised by my remark and looks slightly confused. Finally, he came to his senses just as I pick up my now empty cup.

"You don't have to do that," he quickly says as he grabs my hand gently to stop me from moving.

We stare at each other for a solid minute as he manages to loosen my grip from the plate.

"I can take care of that," he smiles, enchanting me in the moment.

This encounter is the second time now that I am at a loss for words. It has to be something about Darren's gentle nature, or it might be the fact that my interactions with guys are slim to none. He grabs the plate from my hands, never breaking eye contact with me.

"You are the mistress of the household now. I can't have you take my job away from me. For now, anyway." He says as his lip quirks up mischievously before walking away.

I'm so flustered I could scream. My face grew hot as I sit back to replay what Darren said in my mind. The guilt is starting to eat at me again. If I am going to sell the manor, then Darren would lose his job and home. However, I have to be realistic here. This place was too big for me. Not to mention, I don't have the financial means to keep paying Darren, or whoever else lives here. My father probably set up an account for them before he died, and it might be running out. This possible situation only meant two things; I have to do something with the manor soon, and I can't get attached to anything or anyone.

When I finally decide to leave the study, I shove the box back into the drawer of the desk. I will figure everything out tomorrow. Trying to tackle all of this is too much for one day. Slowly, I shut the door behind me and make my way to the foyer to wait for Darren. I am dreading the fact that I am going to have Darren in my car. Besides Amy and my mother, no one else was ever in my car, and I honestly didn't want to deal with any judgmental looks today. I knew my car is old, but no one else would understand.

I guess what I am wearing was acceptable for grocery shopping, but I want to grab my phone and wallet before we leave. As I round the corner, I bump into something hard, like a pole or statue.

Blinking, I took a step back and came face to face with a stranger. He is tall and super thin. His hair is whiter than snow and looks like he could be a hundred years old. Maybe two. I swallow hard as my heart races nervously, and I take another step back.

"I'm so sorry," I stammer.

He bows to me without saying anything at first. As he stands up straight, he grins at me from ear to ear. "It's quite alright, madam. You must forgive this old man. I wasn't watching where I was going."

I've never been bowed to before and don't know how to react; this is the second time in one day. I stand there, awkwardly and shrug my shoulders.

"It's not a problem. It was an accident," I smile.

The older gentleman nods and stares at me for a moment. He opens his mouth as if he is going to speak, but Darren cuts him off. "Reginald! I see you finally met our new mistress."

Darren quickly changed into regular clothing. He is wearing a pair of blue jeans and a black t-shirt with a park of black boots. He looks like some wannabe biker bad boy. For some strange reason, it suits him.

Reginald's warm voice brings me back to my senses as I look at him while he speaks. "I had a feeling this was our new mistress. She has the young master's eyes," he grins.

He must be referring to my father because I am unaware of any other 'young master' that might be in his home.

Reginald began to bow again to show gratitude, and I quickly shake my head and wave my hands to stop him. "Please! You don't have to bow to me. I'm not that kind of person, and besides, it makes me feel uncomfortable."

Reginald looks taken aback. "Not the kind of person?! With all due respect, ma'am, you deserve nothing but the highest respect. It is your god-given right, your birthright!" He boasts with much pride.

I am pretty sure that sweet Reginald is probably losing his marbles, which makes the reality of selling the manor even harder.

Darren is growing uncomfortable and steps between us. He places a gentle hand on my shoulder and starts to push me towards the front door. "Reginald has a lot of work to do. Don't you, Reginald?"

The older man blinks and then nods as if he suddenly realized what is going on. "Oh, yes. I have to dust and reorganize the library again," he laughs, mostly to himself as he hurries away.

Was everyone in this place crazy? They all act as if it is a different era. What is Reginald saying about my birthright? I try to keep my swarming head full of questions at bay as I rush to my room and grab my shoes. Darren rushes me out the door, and I realize I forgot my phone and wallet. I only hope Amy understands about any text message delays.

"We better hurry before it starts to rain. If there is one thing I don't tolerate, it's a wet floor after it rains," Darren sighs.

I say nothing as he pulls keys from his pocket and presses one of the buttons. A loud beep and the roar of an engine come from the side of the building. Curiosity gets me, and I follow Darren to the sound. There is a dip in the wall revealing a covered carport that sits back from the front of the home.

A sleek, black, four-door, BMW hums softly as we approach. The car is so shiny that it looks showroom new. Was this his car?! The more I am learning about Darren and the manor, the more confused I become.

"Is this yours?" I ask with an impressed smile.

Darren chuckles, his eyes looking at my face in amusement.

"No. It's yours. This car was used to take your father around town. Now that you are the new owner, this is yours," he explains.

I am in complete shock. I don't think my mouth can close anymore. It's bad enough that I have the manor but now this car? Just what did my father do in life?

Darren opens the back passenger door and makes me sit in the back. He wouldn't let me sit in the front and argued with me, saying that a proper young lady doesn't sit in the front seat. He needs a news flash because this is the 21st century, and I have every right to sit in the front.

I did my best to not argue with him and keep my eyes on the trees that slide by in my window. The tall oak trees tower over the tiny car as he continues to drive and stop at a stop sign.

"Darren...what was my father?" I ask absentmindedly.

The question hung thick in the air. I can see out of the corner of my eye that his hands tense around the steering wheel. His knuckles turn white as he looks back to me through the review mirror.

"I don't know what you mean," he replies, keeping his eyes on mine.

For a moment, I begin to worry as he didn't look at the road once. He keeps his eyes on mine and manages to keep the car steady down the highway.

I try looking away by shrugging my shoulder, moving my body closer to the front seats. I lean in the middle of them silently, wishing Darren will look back at the road. To my luck, he focuses again on what is in front of him when I got comfortable.

"You know, what was he? What was his job? To be able to afford a manor, fine cars, and to have hired help, it's hard to believe he was able to afford it in this small town," I explain.

Darren relaxes, and the thick, awkward blanket that surrounds us slowly disappears.

"I'm surprised you didn't ask earlier. Your father was a very successful politician. He worked in the town hall and eventually worked his way up to congress. He specialized in human rights and the environment. That was where he met your mother. I don't know all the details, but I'm certain it was there. Soon your father came into some financial investments and bought the manor."

I let out a silent breath of relief now that the fear of my father being a mob boss is gone. It makes sense now, but one thing that I didn't understand was why he still left. For the remainder of the drive, I keep my mouth shut, not wanting to add any more awkward moments. I settle back into my seat eventually, and my eyes examine all the tall buildings that fly past my window.

FIVE

The entire ride to the grocery store is painfully quiet. Darren didn't say two words to me after I stopped asking about my father. As soon as the car is in a parking spot, he hops out and opens my door. It catches me off guard, and I didn't know how to respond.

"Um, thanks," I say quietly.

Darren only curtly nods.

We walk in silence into the store. Darren grabs a cart and pulls out a shopping list from his back pocket. Trying to break the silence between us, I give him a small smile. "So why did you change clothes?"

Slowly he pushes the cart down an aisle and begins to grab items that are needed. "Well, I highly doubt a butler suit would be appropriate in public," he earnestly smirks.

I nod, knowing that he is probably right. A suit

would cause too much attention. As if it wasn't shocking enough to have a father leave a manor behind for their abandoned daughter. To be walking around with someone in a suit would be too much for me today.

Just as we were about to turn the corner of the pasta aisle, I am grabbed from behind. Long, thin arms firmly hold onto me. I squirm a little in panic as the air leaves my lungs. Darren swiftly moves to my side and raises a hand to strike the attacker but stops.

"Lizzy! What a coincidence that I would bump into you here!"

A smile crosses my face as my fleeting moment of panic starts to subside. I recognize the voice instantly and begin to wiggle from her grasp.

"Amy! What are you doing here?"

I'm happy and relieved to see my best friend. It feels like its years, but it was only a couple of weeks since I last saw her.

Amy grins and pushes her bangs from her short, blonde hair and places her hands on her hips. "I just got into town and wanted to buy snacks for tonight. We're still watching a movie later, right?"

"Yeah, we still can. I'm not at the hotel, though. Actually, there's a lot we need to talk about." I almost forgot about the plans I promised her. With trying to get things situated with my mom's house and school, I kind of neglected her. It was the reason why I asked her to come to Virginia so we could spend some time with each other.

Amy smiles brightly as her blue eyes slowly shift to Darren. I can just feel the parade of questions I am going to receive. Darren stares back at her in almost disgust but smiles when I look at him.

"Oh, this is Darren. And this is Amy," I explain, introducing the two of them.

Darren smiles even more and nods. "Pleasure to meet you. Madam, why don't you catch up with your friend, and I will gather the groceries for tonight."

Even though Darren is confusing, I am thankful for some alone time with Amy. There is so much I want to tell her, and I feel like I am going to explode.

When Darren walks out of sight, Amy gasps and grabs my arm, squeezing it gently. "Oh, my stars. Is he your boyfriend?" She gushes.

I want to choke on air. Amy smiles and starts to laugh as I stare at her dumbfoundedly. There would be no way I would be with someone like Darren. He's too stiff and proper. I have a theory that he was brainwashed at some point, perhaps during his childhood. The poor guy probably didn't know how to have fun.

Other shoppers are starting to stare at us as we continue to stand in the middle of the aisle. I quickly grab her arm and pull her towards a meat cooler. Once we are out of the way, I indulge Amy in all the details. The will, the manor, Reginald, and even Darren. Her eyes grew large, like big blue saucers. Her smile grew bigger and bigger with each passing word.

"Oh, wow! To think you were a princess this whole

time!" She laughs.

I smile and start to chuckle, "I hardly doubt that."

"You seem to be in better spirits," a male voice calls out.

Darren startles me. I peer up at him as he held the grocery bags. I give a side glance to Amy and smile. "Yeah, I am now."

"Excellent. Why don't you have your friend join us for dinner? I made sure to grab enough ingredients," he offers, holding up a white plastic bag.

I'm not sure if I like this idea. I'm still trying to get used to the manor, and I'm sure Amy would be overwhelmed.

Before I have a chance to object to the idea, Amy already answers for me.

"I would love to come for dinner."

Darren gives a small nod of his head and turns to me, "Good. Let us return home so your friend can get settled in."

I'm in defeat and just follow behind them as we all left the store. When we arrive at the manor, Amy couldn't hide her excitement as we walk through the threshold. She looks at all the paintings and points out a boar's head by the staircase that I didn't notice.

Darren excuses himself to make dinner and leaves us in the foyer. We watch as he vanishes through a door to the left of the staircase, and when the door opens, I catch a glimpse of a table, but the door shut too fast to see anything else.

Amy is silent for a moment and looks over at me

with a mischievous grin, "I don't like him, he's too uptight," she comments.

I shrug my shoulder. "Darren's nice, but he's a little strange."

An impulse takes over me as I turn to Amy. Maybe staying here instead of a hotel was the best option. I don't have to worry about bedbugs as I previously fretted. From what I can see, Darren did an excellent job keeping the place clean. And with Amy staying here, it will make me feel more at ease. "Why don't you stay here with me? It will make being here a little more bearable. I could use a familiar presence while I figure things out."

Amy looks worried and touches my arm, "Are you going to sell the manor?" She asks.

I dart my eyes away from her gaze. "I'm not sure yet. A lot happened in one day. I just packed up and sold one house, and now I must do it all over again. I just need time to process that first before I can take on another task like that."

Amy looks relieved and lets go of my arm. "Yeah, I would take some time. Who knows, maybe this place will grow on you. How about we get ready for dinner? I want to shower and change from my long drive," she yawns and walks away towards the staircase.

I follow her up the stairs and make a left as she makes a right. I get halfway to my room when I stop and realize that I never told her what room to go to. I turn around and watch her disappear into a room. Amy can be extremely picky and probably wants to explore different room options. If she didn't like any of them, she would let me know

I didn't see Amy until dinner time, and dinner was anything but boring. We ate our food in the dining room. I didn't have a chance to admire the long, dark table or the paintings as Amy took overall conversations, so there were no awkward pauses throughout the night. Darren joined us for a few minutes and smiled at the stories of our college shenanigans. However, I could tell he wasn't genuinely interested. Hearing the same drunk tale, but at different locations, can only be interesting the first three times.

When dinner is over, Amy and I go our separate ways as the day's energy is completely drained from our bodies. The mattress is soft like a cloud and relaxes my muscles, but nothing can stop my racing mind. Every time I close my eyes, I keep thinking that I am back in a motel room and not in this fancy manor. This all had to be some sort of joke. How can someone be so respected by colleagues and claim that they care when they made no effort to keep communication with their family? Only to leave a manor behind for their kid?

The events leading up to today have me so stressed that I see stars. I keep tossing and turning in my overly sized bed and can't get comfortable. After lying down for a few more minutes, I decide that I need some fresh air. Maybe then my tired mind can relax.

The old, wood floor creaks loudly under my feet, making me wince with every step I take. It is well after midnight, and I'm sure everyone is asleep. I would hate myself if I woke Reginald or Amy. Darren, on the other hand, he deserved it. How he slammed the door in my face before letting me speak and insisted that I stay in the manor. It might not have been against my will, but it was still irritating. Even though he made a fantastic dinner, I'm still angry with him.

Luckily, I have Amy here with me, so staying in this monstrosity wouldn't be horrible. She is more than eager to stay in the manor, which didn't surprise me. She always talked about her wealthy family and the large home she grew up in. This manor probably reminds her of her home, and here I thought she might be overwhelmed.

The floors are as cold as they are noisy. My toes feel like they will gain frostbite and fall off any second. I agree with myself that maybe going outside my warm room is a bad idea. Looking at the large stained-glass window in the hallway only proves how cold and rainy it is outside. The notion of going out for fresh air is now terminated, I have no intentions of getting sick.

My stomach turns slightly, letting the gasses rumble throughout my core. It is growling with such vigor that I immediately forgot about my cold feet. "Maybe a snack and then right back to bed," I whisper to myself.

I try hard to ignore the creepy stares from the large paintings of children with halos and wings watching my every move. Whatever they are, they're scary looking in the dark. When I start selling things from the manor, those paintings are the first to go. These hallways are barely lit by the single lightbulbs that are scattered along the wall. This manor has many old antiques that it could be a museum. Everything here has to be about a hundred years old or at least looks that way. It didn't matter. As soon as I get things in order, I'm selling this bleak reminder of my father. There is no way I need a manor to myself. Hopefully, some celebrities will buy it, and that will be the end of it.

It takes me a while to catch my barring's and find the grand staircase that leads to the foyer. The large, oriental rug warms my feet the second I step on it as I try to figure out where the kitchen is. Darren was going through the layout so quick today that I didn't have a chance to ask questions. Everywhere I look is dark and the only light I can see is the lightning flashing through the windows periodically.

I am about to give up and go back to bed when the light from under the kitchen door grabs my attention. Curiosity got the best of me, and I slowly walk to the door. The closer I go to the door, the louder I can hear voices.

Darren's voice is a clear giveaway. He has this raspy accent that was from Ireland or Scotland. When I asked him early today where he was from, he didn't answer me. He had a bad habit of ignoring questions about his personal life and anything else I asked about for that matter. It is starting to become annoying.

The closer I get to the door, I can hear him arguing with someone. The other voice is from a female. I didn't recognize her as she has a thick accent, as well. It sounds something similar to Darren's but has a little twang to it. Australian perhaps?

"This is not up for debate."

"We need her, Darren! If he takes over, we are all good as dead!"

"She will be in danger."

"She will be in danger no matter what choice she makes," the woman retorts.

There's a short silence, and Darren sighs.

"You know I'm right, Darren," she urges.

There is more silence, and I can hear only soft murmurs as I lean my ear closer to the door. The floor creaks beneath me, and instantly I want to run back to bed.

After a long, agonizing moment of silence, there are footsteps, and the door opens slowly. Darren is standing before me as the light from the kitchen floods around him, making him seem like some heavenly being. However, the annoying expression and a slight smile on his lips show me more of a devil. Does he get some sick thrill of catching me off guard?

Clearing my throat, I stand up straight while fixing my NYCU shirt from bunching up in the front.

"Can I help you with something, Miss?" He asks, raising an eyebrow.

My eyes dart over his shoulder to nonchalantly see who the female voice belongs to, but there is no one else in the kitchen.

"Elizabeth?"

"Sorry. I got hungry and was hoping to get some crackers or something." I don't know why I should be nervous about being caught; it wasn't like I did something wrong.

Darren smiles and holds the kitchen door open for me. I walk past him and into the blinding white light. When my eyes finally adjust to the lighting, I see that the kitchen is modern, unlike the rest of the manor. A stainless-steel fridge stands off to the right of the kitchen with a matching stove on the opposite side. Along the wall, there is a long black marble countertop to offset the pure white cabinets.

A wooden island sits in the middle of the room with three chairs on either side. This kitchen looks like it could be used on one of those cooking shows.

"Sit down, Elizabeth. I'll make you a snack," Darren says smoothly as he seems to glide around the kitchen, knowing exactly where everything is.

I compel myself to sit down onto one of the wooden chairs as I watch him get to work. I'm too transfixed by what he is doing that I didn't realize a sandwich, on a plate, is placed in front of me. I star at it intently for a moment and see it is a peanut butter and jelly sandwich with the crust cut off. I think I'm more tired than I thought I was if I couldn't pay attention to him making a simple sandwich.

Slowly I pick up a half and take a bite, letting the sweet, gooey peanut and jelly mixture slowly slide down my throat. Until it got stuck. I cough softly, trying to get it to move, but the lump doesn't budge. Darren is quick to provide me with a small glass of milk, to which I am grateful.

Quickly I take a gulp of the liquid, and instantly the peanut butter dislodges from my throat. I let out a huff now that I can breathe again.

"Thanks," I sheepishly smile.

Darren grins. "You're welcome." Slowly he turns back to the sink and gets to work cleaning the dishes.

As I pick up my sandwich again, I stare at his back, watching his shoulders move as he works. My gaze eventually turns to a door on the other side of the room that looks like it leads to the outside. I wonder if the woman he was talking to left through that door. Or maybe I am just hearing things?

"So, who was that lady?" I question.

Instantly he stops washing the dish he has in his hands, and his shoulders tense slightly.

"What do you mean?" He asks, not turning around to my gaze.

Oh. So now he wants to play dumb.

"I heard you talking to a woman…" my voice trails off as I try to get him to confess.

"You must be mistaken, Elizabeth. I was here by myself. Preparing a list for more grocery shopping tomorrow. You must be imagining things," he says evenly, never once shifting around to look at me.

I knew what I heard. Darren was definitely talking to a woman. I am sure of it. If he was, why would he hide it? Maybe it was his girlfriend? If it is, who were they talking about being in danger?

I decide to leave the conversation alone for the time being. I don't want to start any issues on my first night here.

"Maybe you're right," I shrug.

Finishing my sandwich, I sigh, "You know you don't have to call me Elizabeth. Lizzy is just fine." I hate being called Elizabeth, it makes me sound like an old lady.

Darren shut off the water and grabs a towel to dry off his hands.

"Well, 'Elizabeth' is your birth name; therefore, I shall call you as such. I'll never understand the fascination with young girls to butcher their namesakes to something completely different," he teases as he turns to look at me.

Blinking, I finish my milk and take the plate to the sink. "Young girl? You're not that much older than me, you know," I challenge.

Darren watches me from the corner of his eye as I gather up the sponge, he was just using so I can wash my dish. He is quiet for a long time before his face broke into a strained, crooked grin.

"I guarantee I am much older than you are," he states.

I ignore him as I rinse off the dish and put it on the dish rack to dry.

"You know, this is supposed to be my job," he taunts as he grabs a towel to dry the dish I just washed.

As he picks it up, I sigh, "My mom was always working, so I did the dishes as long as she did the laundry. I hate folding clothes. However, when she was working late, I had to do everything on my own anyway. I'm not used to having a butler wait on me hand and foot like this."

Darren nods. "I'm sorry about your mother. My mother died when I was a boy. My father tried to raise me, but one day he decided to leave, and I found myself all alone. Or, from what I was told. I was too young when it all happened, and I don't remember much."

I look at him and see the teasing smile he had is now replaced with a look of pure sadness. The expression stays only for a moment because his eyes glance at mine, and a small smile erupts on his face.

"Seems like we have something in common." He adds. He is trying to joke, but I'm not buying it. For a split second there, I caught his moment of weakness, but I wouldn't dare bring it back up.

"Yeah, but at least you knew you had a father for a brief time. My father left us before I was born. The only thing I really know of him is that he was well-liked apparently, and he must have been rich because look at this place!" I say, waving my hands around my head at the vast kitchen ceilings.

Darren silently agrees and slowly puts the towel down and places the dish back into the cabinet above his head. "Yes, but your father was a good man, Elizabeth. Always remember that."

I don't know what it is, but the way he talks about his own father abandoning him makes me feel a little uneasy. Like, maybe I shouldn't have said anything about mine at all because now it's awkwardly silent.

I didn't get the chance to say anything else stupid as Darren breaks the silence by pointing to the clock on the wall.

"I believe it's time we go to bed. A young lady shouldn't be up so late, it will cause wrinkles around your eyes if you don't get enough sleep."

His mood swings on this emotion boat are starting to make me seasick. And who even says things like that anymore? He sounds like a little old lady, but his words held some truth. I am exhausted, and now that I had my snack, I am ready for bed. It was best if I left our conversation the way it is, I didn't want to make it even weirder between us.

"Good idea. I'm drained from moving boxes and traveling so much. I guess I'll see you in the morning," I smile.

"Goodnight, Elizabeth."

"Goodnight, Darren."

It takes a moment for my eyes to adjust to the darkness in the foyer so I can make my way back to my room. As I close the door behind me, I yawn loudly and rub the heels of my hands into my eyes gently. There is too much to do and not enough time to complete everything. I fear I won't have everything finished in time for me to return to the city.

The manor is too big, and I only broke the tip of the iceberg going through my father's study. There are still many rooms, and I just half hoped that they are empty. My body starts to ache with the desire to lay back down on the delicate mattress. It was probably made of goose feathers or something fancy like in the rest of the manor. Whatever the case, it's comfortable. My brain finally allows my eyes to close and wander into a more profound slumber.

I still can't shake the feeling that Darren is still hiding things from me. I know I've only been here a day, but there is something about Darren that bothers me, and I just can't put my finger on it. Maybe I'm just tired and reading into everything too much. Mom used to poke fun of how much of a worrier I was, but I can't ignore the rock that is currently in my stomach.

SIX

The next day all the rain that came rolling through the night before is gone, and what is left is a sunny, beautiful morning. It was too gorgeous to not eat outside. Darren was kind enough to accommodate my request and clean the white, iron table and chairs.

Amy meets me downstairs, so Darren can walk us outside. He leads us to the door that is on the right-hand side of the staircase. The door opens to a sunroom that acts as a mini-greenhouse with another door leading to the gardens.

The sun is warm on my skin, and the breeze carries the smell of Haciendas in the air. Amy and I sit down at the metal table and look at the massive garden as Darren serves breakfast. He asked me earlier what I wanted to eat, and I requested something simple, like an omelet or pancakes. Darren must have misheard me as he brings out trays of bacon, eggs made three different ways, toast, and pancakes. There is no way that Amy and I can eat all of this food.

I shouldn't be surprised, dinner the night before was just as extravagant, but I still sat there with a bewildered look on my face.

As Darren pours orange juice in my glass, Amy smiles at me in delight, "Oh Lizzy! How can you beat this view and this service? I really think you should just keep the manor!" She insists as she helps herself to some bacon.

"The manor is too big for one person. Besides, Amy tells me you just graduated from school. I'm sure you will want to find a job in the city or explore the world," Darren says as he places the pitcher of juice in the middle of the table.

Darren is right. It hasn't been that long since we graduated. I was too focused on trying to get mom's house in order; I forgot how to live my life. I wonder what mom would say if she knew I was left with a manor as big as three houses. She would probably laugh or urge me to keep it. If there were two things in life my mother wanted, it was a roof over my head and food in my stomach. Here, I have both.

"I haven't decided what I want to do. I appreciate you two giving me insight, but I need to figure this out for myself," I state firmly. To be honest, I am starting to get irritated with the two of them. Both are trying to convince me one way or the other. I would much rather figure things out for myself.

Darren takes some empty plates. "You are correct,

Miss. Elizabeth, you can take as much time as you need."

I happen to take a glance at Amy as she eats her toast, and if looks could kill, Darren would be six feet under. To relieve the tension, I clear my throat and wiggle my hand at the blonde in front of me.

"Hey, since we have some time to ourselves, did you want to do something tonight?"

Amy taps a finger to her lips as she thinks for a moment. "We could watch a movie," she suggests shrugging a shoulder.

I almost want to laugh. Amy is the life of the party, and she just wants to watch a movie?

"No! We didn't get to celebrate our graduation properly. There's a new club in town, well at least I think it's new, called Viper? I think we should check it out," I recommend.

It's been too long since I went out to dance or have a good time. Not to mention, I hardly had any time with Amy since my mother's death. After everything that happened, even I needed to go out and let loose a little.

"Come on, we can go to the mall and get outfits. I'll even buy you the first drink," I coax.

For some reason, Amy looks concerned and glances at Darren, who says nothing and saunters away. After a while, she agrees. "Okay. If you want to go to Viper, we can go."

"Great! Let's get going and try to find some cute outfits for tonight," I beam.

I can't stop grinning as we finish our breakfast. Going out tonight is the real stress relief I need. I also want to repay Amy for all the emotional help she is. I feel like I took away some of her fun in the past weeks when she tried to get me to go out. It is only right that I try to make it up to her.

*

The mall isn't packed during the day, and we find a parking spot close to the doors. Amy insists that we take her car since it's newer, and my car would most likely leave us stranded. I laugh silently to myself because I knew it is true. My car is so old that I could probably pass it off as an antique.

It is nice to go out with Amy and keep my mind off the manor. Thankfully she didn't mention any of it while we walked through different shops.

"Come on, Lizzy. Pick something so we can get ready," Amy whines.

One thing Amy hates is my indecisive nature, I knew this, but it didn't stop me from second-guessing every option I pick. I would choose something and feel good about it but put it back because I was unsure.

"I'm looking. I don't want to spend a lot of money on a dress." I whine back, and we both laugh.

"Here, I'll help." She offers.

The two of us rummage through the racks of clothes, in the woman's department store, to find the perfect dress.

"Here, what about this?" She smiles, pulling a short, black dress with one sleeve off of the rack. I'm not sure just by looking at the dress. It seems too skinny and tight.

"Come on, try it on," she pleads.

Sighing, I grab the dress from her and walk into the dressing room. After getting undressed, I slipped the fabric over my head and shoved my arm through the left, and only, sleeve. Once I pull down the material to the middle of my thighs, I was impressed with how the dress fit.

The fabric is smooth like velvet, and it's classy. The dress goes well with my figure and looks good against my chestnut brown hair. A bang on my dressing room door startles me as Amy's voice rings throughout the hallowed room.

"Hey! I want to see it! Don't tell me you took it off already!"

I grunt softly and unlock my door to show her the dress, smoothing down the sides as I step out.

Amy gives a low whistle and twirls her finger. "Do a little turn for me," she teases. Rolling my eyes, I did as she asks and slowly turn around in a circle. Amy claps her hands together with excitement, *"C'est Magnifique!"*

I laugh until I see the price tag. My heart drops, and all the color drains from my face. This dress is over my budget, there is no way I can afford it.

"Amy," I whisper, taking a quick look around to make sure none of the workers can hear me. "This dress is expensive; I'm not going to be able to pay for it."

The dress looks so good on me, and now it's out of my reach. Talk about a mood killer. I didn't have a chance to wallow in self-pity as Amy clicks her tongue and tears the price tag off.

"Go into the dressing room and change, I will buy the dress for you." She commands.

My eyes widen as far as they can go, there is no way I am going to let her pay for it! Amy shakes her head and places a finger on my lips as if she knew what I am going to say.

"Don't even think about it. This is my graduation gift to you," she says sternly, her bright blue eyes staring at me intensely.

Without another word, she walks away to the front register. Her blonde, pixie cut head bobbing around the racks until she gets in line. I smile to myself as I shut my dressing room door. I am genuinely thankful to have a friend like Amy. She is always there to look out for me and makes sure I a, taken care of. I'll have to remember to get her a killer Christmas gift now.

After I am dressed back into my clothes, I walk out to meet Amy with a shopping bag in hand. Carefully she puts the dress into the bag and hands it over to me. I grab the thin handles and stare down at it for a minute.

"Amy, you really didn't have to do that," I start, but Amy only grins and wraps an arm around my shoulders, giving me a small squeeze.

"Lizzy, I wanted to. It's a gift from me to you. Besides, if we took any longer, the mall would close with us inside," she giggles.

"Thank you, Amy. I am grateful to have a friend like you."

"Likewise. Now, onward to the club!" She cheers.

SEVEN

It didn't take us long to get ready once we were home. My hair is simple with a little, wavy curl at the end, and I put on some light makeup. I want to try and keep my look classy to go along with my dress.

Darren says nothing at first when he sees us. He stares for a while before opening the door with a smile and wishing us to have fun. He is acting strange. Well, stranger than yesterday. Ever since Amy and I agreed to go out this morning, he was keeping his distance for most of the day. If he wanted to come out with us, he could have asked. Although trying to picture someone like Darren at a club only makes me laugh in my head. He probably wouldn't dance and stay close to the wall all night, a complete wallflower.

Amy drives us to the club and parks on a side street. I am nervous about our little adventure tonight, and it's making my pulse race. The chilly breeze is welcomed on my flush face as I try everything to stay calm. I'm not exactly an ace getting into clubs being underage. I don't turn twenty-one for another few weeks, so I have to rely on Amy to get us into clubs. She would flirt with the bouncers or come up with a story to get us into the building every time. It got to the point where the staff knew Amy well enough to just let us in. However, this was in New York, with a new club in a different state, I'm not sure how she is going to pull this off.

My pulse begins to beat faster as panic heightens in my heart, and I grab Amy's arm without thinking. Her shiny sequin red dress nearly blinds me under the lamplight as she quickly turns around to look at me.

"I think this is a bad idea, we're going to get caught this time," I plead. I also start to feel bad because if we get caught, it will be my fault. This excursion was my idea in the first place.

Amy smiles and places a hand on mine. "You say this every time, and guess what? We have yet to get caught. Don't worry about it," she calmly says as she begins to pull me along with her once more.

Sure, I get scared every single time we did this, but it's always a thrill when we succeed. Of course, Amy goes out a lot more than me, she is gone practically every night. For some reason, this time is different. I think it has something to do with me being in my hometown and across the street from the lawyer's office. It's like I'm afraid of bumping into someone that might know me.

As we get closer to the front doors, my hands itch

and grow clammy. A bouncer is standing in the doorway wearing a black T-shirt with Viper spray painted in neon green across the chest. He is wearing so much black that he blends in with the dark building behind him. Amy strolls up to the bouncer with confidence as I stay close next to her. The bouncer looks at us for a long moment and holds out a hand. "ID, please," he grunts.

I watch as Amy search through her tiny purse and pretends to look for her ID. After a few minutes, she pouts and gazes up at the burly bouncer. "Oh no, I can't find it. I must have left it at home," she frowns.

The bouncer is unphased as he held out his hand a little longer and then crosses his arms over his chest. I watch as his muscles flex under his tight shirt from irritation. "Sorry. No ID, no entry," he huffs.

Amy isn't one to give up easily. Gently she lays her hand on the bouncer's arm, stroking her thumb on his skin. "I'll make a deal with you. If you let us in for one hour, I promise we will leave right away," she coos, using her friendly charm to win him over. Amy has this way with men. I've seen her do it multiple times, she would sweet talk them, and it was like they were under a spell. I wish I had half of the confidence she has.

The bouncer slowly breaks in to smile as he stares into her eyes. Slowly, he reaches down and lifts the red velvet rope to let us in. "One hour," he teases with a love-drunk smile.

Amy grins in success and pats his elbow. "One hour," she winks and grabs my hand. Quickly, I'm pulled past the bouncer and through the threshold. Amy needed only one look and a smile, and she could get herself out of any situation. The girl amazes me sometimes.

The loud bass of the music drums through my chest, drowning my thoughts and anxieties with the motions. The dance floor is full, and the bar proves to be challenging to get to. I manage to get through the swarm of people, with Amy at my side, to a couple of free bar stools.

"Isn't this fun?" Amy yells over the sound of loud techno music.

The bar is dark with green glow sticks on the back mirror, and strobing lights flashing brightly in the corners of my eyes. It's a little too much for my senses, and I pray that Amy only wants to stay an hour.

"Yeah, this is a blast!" I lie, not wanting to be the wet blanket.

"What can I get you, ladies?"

A male voice cuts through the booming base and gets our attention. The bartender's gold name tag glitters in the neon lights against his black shirt. Amy puckers her lips a little and leans in to read his name.

"Can we get two specials, Jesse?" She requests.

A sweet smile crosses his face as he pushes his long, brown hair out of the way and grabs a bottle. "Of course. Two specials, coming up."

I am mesmerized as I watch his tattooed arms get to work. He pours three different liquids into two cups, swirls them around with ice, and places cherries on top.

"Here you go." He gently places the glasses in front of us.

"Thank you," Amy smiles, handing Jesse a twenty-dollar bill. "Oh, and keep the change."

I take my drink and sip on it slowly, letting the warm feeling fill my stomach. Right now is a time to forget about the heartache of selling my childhood home and to let go of the lingering anger I have for my father. There is nothing more I want than to relax and enjoy my time with Amy.

Amy already finishes her drink and leans into me so I can hear her over the loud music. The way she can drink and not get hungover always surprises me. "Don't look now, but a total hottie is looking at you," she whispers in my ear.

Carefully I observe my surroundings and lock eyes with a guy who is staring at me from across the bar. My cheeks grow hot, and I quickly avert my eyes, focusing on Amy.

"Yeah, I can see that," I grimace and down the rest of my drink. The alcohol settles to the bottom of my glass and burns down my throat as I try to get my courage out of my stomach. "Amy, you know I'm not very good with guys. They find me boring," I scoff.

"Well, you seem to talk to Darren, okay," she comments with a pleasant smile.

My ears turn red and burn from embarrassment, or maybe the alcohol, I'm not sure. Darren is the last name I want to hear right now. I give Amy a sour look that only makes her laugh. Slowly, I smile and shrug my shoulders.

"Darren confuses me. One moment he acts so proper like he is from a different time, and then he changes. He gets distant and ignores my questions. The man is too hot and cold for my liking," I sigh, eating my gin-soaked, cherry garnish off the toothpick.

Amy laughs as she plays with her empty glass. When she is finished, she eats the cherry off the toothpick like I did and pushes the cup towards the bartender.

"Look, I know you've been through a lot. To go through the motions of your mother passing and now finding out you have a manor, you need to take some time for yourself. Live a little. Let your heart open up, you never know what will happen." She says in a sing-song voice.

In some ways, Amy is right. I did go through hell with school, my mother's death, and now trying to figure out this manor issue. Tonight is my night to let loose and have fun. There should be no worries in my world. If I sell some items in the manor, I can pay off my mother's medical debt with no issue. So, in all reality, I have nothing to worry about, I always have a plan.

"You know, Amy. You're right. I need to start having fun again and not worry so much." I say with determination.

We giggle and slowly get up from our stools to go to the dance floor, but I stop when I feel a light tap on my shoulder. I freeze and look over my shoulder to see the handsome stranger from across the bar. He has dark eyes and deep, mahogany hair. His baby face and bright smile are enough to make me swoon.

"Hello. I know this may seem odd, but I couldn't let you walk away without buying you a drink first," the handsome stranger grins.

Out of the corner of my eye, I watch Amy slowly step away to give me some space. I look up at him and smile. "Sure. One drink. I'm Elizabeth, but everyone calls me Lizzy." I nervously introduce myself and hold out my hand to shake his.

My anxiety is spiking as my body goes into autopilot. I could bang my head against the bar for acting like such an oddball. Who the hell shakes hand with anyone at the club?! Darren's old fashion attitude is starting to rub off on me.

"I'm Luke. It's a pleasure to meet you, Lizzy," he chuckles and shakes my hand gently, seeming to be unphased by the odd gesture. His skin is warm and soft, with a firm grip. As soon as he lets go, he waves down the bartender to get two more drinks. I take advantage of this moment to look and see where Amy went to. I scan the crowd and begin to worry that I can't see her. The loud thumping of the music's bass is keeping me from concentrating on Amy's whereabouts.

Luke pokes my shoulder with a smile. "Here."

I smile, seeing him holding two dark-colored drinks for us. A strong smell wafts from my glass, making me wrinkle my nose. I don't want to be rude and quickly drank the whole glass. Hopefully, this would be enough to make me more relax. Luke smirks and finishes his drink before grabbing my empty glass to give to the bartender.

"Would you like to dance?" Luke asks.

"Sure," I enthusiastically yell. Maybe I am *too* relax now.

Luke keeps silent as he rolls up the sleeves of his dark blue button-up and takes my hand to guide me to the dance floor. The bass thumps harder in my chest, the closer we get to the speakers.

Our bodies sway to the upbeat tempo, and for the first time since my life turned crazy, I am having fun. No thoughts ran through my head as my eyes close, and the music takes me away. We dance for a few minutes, and my body starts to slow down. My head starts to spin first. My body feels heavy, and I didn't know I'm falling until Luke's strong arms wrap around me.

"Whoa, looks like you have too much to drink," he muses.

I'm limp, and I can barely open my eyes. Luke's face looks blurry, and my stomach is in knots. When the room stops spinning, I try to stand. Frantically I search for Amy in the sea of people. We have to leave before I embarrass myself and puke on Luke.

"Come on, let's go outside for some fresh air," he says softly and leads me through the crowd.

We sneak by a few patrons and make it through a door that leads into the alleyway. The crisp night air cools down my hot cheeks, making my stomach not hurt as much. Whatever is in those drinks is making my stomach do backflips.

I glace up at Luke with a smile. I'm starting to feel better knowing that someone is here to help me. "Thank you. It's nice to know there are still gentlemen in the world," I manage. Trying to give him a compliment while keeping a calm composure is no easy task.

Luke says nothing and stares at me. The vibe he is giving off is starting to make me sweat as my fight or flight response kicks in. I notice another man enter the opening of the alleyway opposite of us. I'm uneasy as the man walks towards where we are standing.

"Maybe we should go inside. I'm sure Amy is looking for me," I whisper desperately.

I reach for the door handle to go back into the club when Luke grabs my arm. I laugh, thinking he is trying to fool around, but his grip becomes tighter, and he roughly pulls me to the ground.

My head bounces off the blacktop, making a loud cracking sound. My ears ring, and my head throbs as I reach up to feel a warm, wet sensation on my forehead. When I can focus, my hand is covered in blood, and Luke is standing over me, breathing heavily. An audible hiss escapes his throat in frustration as the other stranger finally joins him.

"The drug didn't take. Her body is already filtering it out before I had a chance," Luke growls, reaching into his back pocket for a cellphone.

The pounding in my head is growing, and soon the

sound of my blood rushing pounds in my ears. My eyes flutter closed as the full effect of my head injury takes over my body. I try to move, but my body is numb, and my elbow stings from the fall.

"Why are you doing this?" I wheeze.

Luke and the stranger wickedly smile in unison as Luke crouches down to my level. He reaches out and grabs a fist of my hair to pull my head up. The sting of my fresh wound causes my eyes to water as my heart thumps in fear.

"Simple. We have a job to do, princess. Our boss can't have you waltzing around, now can he?" He sneers.

"Hurry up! You're taking too long!"

"Quiet! I know what I'm doing!" Luke growls.

From the same back pocket, Luke pulls out a black leather handle and presses a button. The spring-loaded device produces a bright gleam of a blade as he holds it to my face. "Any last words?" he menacingly grins, showing off his white teeth and what appears to be fangs.

I'm losing it. This has to be a mixture of pain and fear to make me delusional. My heart is pumping so hard that I knew it would stop this time. Luke raises his arm, with the blade in hand, ready to strike my skin. I quickly close my eyes, wishing that I never mentioned going out tonight. Before the tears can reach my cheeks, the tension on my hair is gone, and I fall back down. The sound of a man's scream, and bones cracking fill my ears when I open my eyes. Darren is holding Luke by the arm, pushing him against the club wall. With what strength I have left, I push myself up to watch Darren squeeze on Luke's neck with his free hand.

"You better give me one good reason why I shouldn't kill you right now," Darren snarls.

Luke coughs and scoffs, "I don't have anything to say to you."

The other man that knew Luke reaches down to grab the knife that fell and starts to run in Darren's direction.

"Darren!"

I can't get up fast enough and fear the worst. Out of nowhere, a blinding red blur came from the alleyway entrance and pummels the attacker to the ground. "Oi! Look what we got here. A snake in the grass."

Amy is standing on the attacker, one heel on his back and the other on his hand. I think it's Amy, the girl looks like Amy, but her voice was different. She has an accent. As I listen to her speak, I soon realize I recognize her voice. It's the same as the woman who was arguing with Darren the other night. What the hell is going on here?!

"You took too long," Darren barks, causing Amy to put her hands on her hips.

"Well, excuse me. There were more than these two inside I had to take care of first," she hisses.

Luke laughs, causing Darren to press harder on his windpipe.

"Now answer me, who sent you. Tell the truth, and

I might let you live," Darren threatens.

"I'm not saying anything. You'll have to kill me, I guess," Luke wheezes.

Amy digs her heel harder into the man's hand on the ground, making him howl in pain. "And what about you? You better talk soon, I'm starting to grow bored," she sneers.

The man looks up at Luke and begins to sweat. Amy presses down on his hand once more, making him yell louder.

"Okay! Okay! We were ordered to kill the girl," he confesses.

"By who?"

"I don't know."

"You don't know? Or you won't say?" Amy questions adding more pressure.

"Ow! We don't know who! All I know is, we were sent a letter and from what I could remember, it said the girl will ruin everything and to take care of her. Please don't kill me," he cries.

I finally had enough of whatever creep show is going on. "Would someone like to explain to me what is going on?" I demand. I would have stomped my foot, but I'm too unsteady, to begin with.

Amy and Darren turn their heads towards me. If I were standing, I would have taken a step back. Both of them have a dangerous look in their eyes, and when Amy tries to speak to me, I can't hear the words. Fangs protrude from her mouth slightly like the man on the ground. I look to Darren and Luke, who also sport the look. I am ultimately terrified.

Luke began to laugh. "What's wrong, princess? You act like you haven't seen a vampire before," he taunts.

Darren hisses and lifts Luke higher against the wall, "Quiet!" He snarls. When Darren glances back at me, and his expression softens, "Elizabeth, we can explain everything," he softly speaks.

At this point, I can't fathom what I just heard or how Darren could explain this. Vampires? Meaning, they are all vampires? This all has to be fake. There were no such things as vampires. They are just monsters in movies and teen books! What did any of this have to do with me? I am overwhelmed, and my head begins to spin again. Soon my world goes dark, and the last thing I hear before succumbing to darkness is my name being called out by Darren.

EIGHT

My legs burn. I ran as fast as I could. Laughter starts to fill my ears as sickening hissing noises follow closely behind. I don't know where I am going, but I'm sure as hell wasn't going to stick around. My head throbs as I try to peer through the darkness. A bright light shimmers ahead of me, and the closer I walk towards it, I can hear the loud but hushed whispers of two people.

Slowly my eyes open, and I realize I wasn't in the alleyway anymore. Instead, I am laying in my bed dressed in my pajamas. I looked at the door to see Darren and Amy arguing.

"I told you not to go to that club. Too many of his followers are out there," Darren hisses quietly.

"Oi! I was following orders. 'Make Lizzy happy' remember? She wanted to go. How was I supposed to know this would happen?!" Amy argues through clenched teeth.

"Not to mention you were negligent! If I didn't get there in time, she would have been dead!"

"If you would have told Lizzy the truth, none of this would have happened!"

They both start to growl at each other flashing their fangs. I blink and sit too fast. The sudden rush of sitting up causes my stomach to lunge slightly. I look at them, thinking that this is all a dream. Vampires are real, and somehow, I am caught in the middle of something still.

The back of my neck pulsates, and I reach up to feel a bandage on the spot where my head hit the concrete. Amy notices I'm sitting up and pushes Darren's arm. "Look, you woke her up."

The way the two of them act, it's like watching a brother and sister fighting. It would have been amusing if I knew the two weren't bloodthirsty monsters.

Amy came closer to me and sits on the edge of the bed, causing me to back away. The hurt expression on her face makes my heart squeeze, but I have no idea what is going on. Until someone starts to explain what happened, I'm not going to get chummy with anyone again.

"We uh, we haven't been telling you the truth," she starts softly.

"Yeah, you think?" I snap.

I am furious with all the secrecy and the fact that Amy never told me who she was. It really makes me question our friendship.

Darren pulls up a chair from the little table by my bed and runs a hand through his hair.

When no one is speaking, I grow impatient.

"Okay, first off, why do you two act like you know each other? Second, what the hell happened last night? Are you guys really vampires, or is this some weird cult fetish?" I ramble.

Amy clears her throat, "To answer the first question, well, I've known Darren for as long as I can remember. My name is really Amaryllis, but I usually go by Amy. I was sent by your father to make sure you stayed safe while in school."

I'm in deep shock. Amy, the one person who I relied on in my messed-up world, isn't who she really is. So, the stories of her wealthy family are nothing but lies? The whole situation is sickening and leaves a bad taste in my mouth.

Darren and Amy reach out for me at the same time, but I pull away again. I'm furious and stare at the two of them for a while before I can speak.

"What else? What else aren't you telling me?" I demand.

Amy looks at Darren and watches as he slumps back into his chair, not saying a word. She huffs and looks at me. "Those men that attacked you last night are working for someone who wants to harm you. Your father was a powerful and influential vampire…"

"Enough, Amaryllis!" Darren snaps.

Amy studies at Darren and barres her teeth. "She needs to know the truth!"

Darren stands up from his chair and stares down at her. "Not like this. She can't handle something like this right now!"

"Oh, like you care!" She retorts.

Darren growls and takes a step towards her. "You are out of line!"

"It's her heritage! She is next in line for the chair!"

"She will be in more danger than she already is now!"

I eventually have enough. It is all too much, the vampires, the fighting, and now there is the talk of a chair? I never grew up in a household with arguing parents before, and now I'm thankful I didn't have to go through it. "Stop it both of you!" I yell and crawl out of bed. My legs wobble slightly, but I struggle at first to gain my balance.

Darren stretches out for my arm, but I push his hand away. There is too much going on, and I can't wrap my brain around it.

"I have a hard time believing you guys are vampires or the fact I am so how involved with some weird mafia hit. Oh, and my father is a vampire?" I laugh in disbelief. Sighing, I ran a hand through my hair, feeling little pieces of asphalt slowly slip from the strands "I need some time to myself."

My body moves quickly past the two of them as they say nothing. My head is reeling with the idea of vampires being real and the fact that I'm stuck in the middle. Is Amy telling the truth? Was my father a vampire? If he was, did that mean I was too? Or was this some messed up coma dream?

When I finally take a deep breath, I find myself outside by the gardens. The dark sky starts to grow lighter with the oncoming morning. I sit down on the stone steps watching the tree branches sway in the cool, early morning breeze. I close my eyes, trying to make sense of all that is happening around me when I hear soft footsteps approaching me. I jump and hastily turn around to see Darren making his way in my direction.

Seeing a familiar face makes me breathe a bit easier, even though I'm still hesitant because of the whole vampire thing. After everything that happened, I'm feeling jumpy and don't know what to expect next. I observed him as he slowly sits down next to me, keeping his own eyes on the flowers and trees. We sit in silence for a while, watching as the sky's dark veil slowly lifts, revealing a soft pink aura.

"You weren't supposed to find out this way," Darren states softly after sitting in silence.

I swallow hard and look at him. "How was I supposed to find out?" I ask evenly.

My heart swarms like an aggravated beehive of emotional betrayal. Strangely, I'm glad Darren is out here with me instead of Amy. She is supposed to be my friend, and instead, she lies to me for four years. I confide in her, I cried on her shoulder, only to find out that she was lying to me.

Darren sighs and ran a hand through his hair. "Your father wanted you to figure out what you were going to do with the manor first, then we were going to tell you."

I bit my lip and glared at him, "Tell me the truth. What is going on here?" I ask, feeling emotionally drained from the night's events.

The look on Darren's face says it all. He is ashamed for lying to me, and more importantly, he looks almost scared to tell me. There is a long pause with nothing but the two of us staring at each other. His eyes trace my face before he looks away, breaking the trance. His shoulders ease up, and for the first time since I met him, he looks normal, using the term loosely. Darren isn't acting like the uptight butler I first met; he is now just a guilty guy.

"Your father, may he rest in peace, was a good man. He wanted to help people and bring peace to everyone, but some people in this world just want destruction. Master Edmund took me in when I didn't have anyone. He did the same with Amaryllis and Reginald. We were society's castaways, and it was him that brought us together like a family. For saving my life, I vowed to serve him in any way possible."

Darren watches the rising sun as I stare at him. He keeps quiet, and I can tell quickly that he misses my father. When I was growing up, I had my mother to help guide me through life. Darren had no one. For some reason now, I'm the one that starts to feel guilty. The words I say in passing about my father earlier probably hurt Darren pretty bad.

"Yes, Amaryllis was sent to your school to protect

you while you were there, but there is something you need to understand Elizabeth. Any orders your father gave us was to protect you." Darren studies me. The fleeting butterfly feeling bubbles from my stomach, making my heart race. I swallow hard and nod, wanting him to continue.

"There is an old vampire legend that when the gods created man, they also created animals, creatures, plants, water, air, things for man to survive, to keep them humble and in check. Your father, among others, was from the bloodline of the first vampire, the Originem. For hundreds of years, your father fought for the safety of humans and vampires. He wanted a world where everyone coexisted. However, that will never be a reality. Humans fear what they don't understand, and the vampire race fears weakness."

I blink as a white-hot flash of fear starts to sink in my heart. Darren sounds convincing, and I can't believe that I am entertaining this nonsense. "If my father was a vampire and part of this bloodline, then why am I not a vampire?"

Darren chuckles at my curiosity. "It's a little more complicated than that. There was a time where vampires of the Originem were changing humans to build the race. It takes more than just a bite. There is a blood sharing ritual where any vampire can turn humans. It started to get out of hand, which leads to the creation of the vampire council. The council was a select few from the Originem that oversaw all vampire activity. They made turning humans to vampires illegal, and any vampire was sentenced to death if they went against the council. Your father was the head of the council until four years ago."

"Shouldn't the vampire race have died out then? If they couldn't create more vampires, then there shouldn't be any left," I say softly.

His laughter surprises me. Darren shakes his head and laughs at me as if I said the funniest thing in the world.

"You watch too many movies Elizabeth," he snickers.

The blood rushes to my face with embarrassment, and the heat creeps to my ears. It took everything in me to not look away from Darren.

"Like every animal or human on earth, we still procreate. It's like genetics. In order for the offspring to be full vampire, both parties must be vampires," he explains.

That would explain why I'm not a vampire. "Okay, but what about the sunlight?"

Again, he laughs and shakes his head no. "We don't die in the sun. Well, anymore. After thousands of years of evolving, we can tolerate the sun. We still have our strength and speed, and before you ask, no, we don't turn into bats. Everything you read, seen or heard is mostly fiction."

The reality of all the information making a little sense was started to weigh on my mind. If there was one thing I was sure of, it was the fact that I knew less about my father now than ever.

I sigh softly in slight frustration, feeling lost in my sea of uncertain emotions. Me? A vampire descendant? Why couldn't it be someone else? Why did this have to be me?

"What do I do now?" I mutter.

Darren shrugs his shoulders and grimaces. He glances away from me and towards the mid-morning sun. "I can't tell you what decision to make Elizabeth. Just know, you need to make a choice soon," he says and shuts his eyes as the sun starts to peek over the trees and onto our faces.

"What do you mean?" I question.

Darren bore holes into my eyes, and his demeanor changes. He looks so stern that it's almost frightening. "There are people within the council that weren't a fan of your father's, and I am more than certain that one of them caused your father's death. The night before your father died, he disclosed to us your existence. Your father broke one of the sacred rules the council created, and someone found out somehow. Elizabeth, someone knows you live, and you have the blood of the Originem, Edmunds blood, pumping through your veins. You are the rightful heir to the head of the council. Vampires will be after you."

I keep silent as I gaze off into the distance. No matter where I go, someone will be after me. All because I exist.

"Elizabeth," Darren's soft voice reaches out to me as his hand grabs mine. "I vow, as long as I am still breathing, to protect you. Reginald, Amaryllis, and I vowed this same oath to your father when he took us in. I may have failed him, but I won't fail you."

His words wash over me and make me feel a little at ease, but it is still unsettling that I am going to be the center of attention. I force a smile at Darren and give his hand a squeeze. "Thank you," is all that I could muster.

"Come, you should get some rest, you hardly had any sleep," he coaxes.

Darren helps me up from the ground and escorts me back inside. The light follows up through the windows and onto the foyer floor. When the door closes, I notice Amy pacing by the stairs. She sees us and stops her frantic back and forth. Our eyes meet, and I can feel my anger slowly start to drift away.

"Lizzy, I am so sorry for not telling you. I just-"

I got her to stop talking by hugging her. It takes her a second to realize what I'm doing, and soon she encloses her arms around me. "It's okay, Amy. I understand now, well sort of. I realize that things are going to get weird and messy, and I'm going to need my best friend to be there for me."

Amy is all that I have left. She's the only family that I have. Sure, I had Aunt Kat, but I'm not as close to her. Amy looks relieved as she leans back and wipes away a tear. Her smile spreads from ear to ear, fangs, and all as she pats my cheek. "Just know that I am always your friend first, bodyguard second," she giggles.

Darren steps up behind me and lays a gentle hand

on my shoulder. "Amaryllis, Miss Elizabeth should get some rest. She had a long night," he warned softly.

I am not about to argue. My body aches, and I am emotionally depleted. Spending a few hours in bed sounds like heaven. I should be thanking my lucky stars that I can walk away from what happened the night before with only a cut on my head and some bruising. I can only imagine how worse it could have been.

I leave Darren and Amy in the foyer and trudge my feet back to my room. My body hurt, craving for the plush, down feather blanket on my California king. The moment my body hits the mattress, my eyes ripple close. The aches and pains slowly melt away as my mind surrenders to complete darkness.

NINE

I'm asleep a lot longer than I want to be. There were a couple of times that I woke up and noticed it was still night out. My body felt like it ran three marathons in one day mixed with having the feeling of brittle bones of an eighty-year-old. I'm also sure I was snoring loudly at one point, as well.

I don't remember when I fell back asleep again or how long it was this time. My slumber is interrupted with the sound of my door being thrown open. It bangs against the wall loudly, making me jump.

"Elizabeth, you need to get up." Darren's low voice drifts to my ears, making me slowly open my eyes. He is standing next to my bed, holding a form-fitting business dress. I groan, sitting up and stare at the dress before looking at him.

"What's that? What time is it?" I moan, trying to figure out what day, time, and the year it is. There is still some crust in my eyes, making it hard for me to open them all the way.

He is more frantic and demanding today than before. I would joke and ask if he saw a ghost but knowing my luck those were real too.

"What's going on?" I yawn, finally wiping the crust from my eyes.

Darren huffs and shuts the door. "The head of the council came for an unscheduled visit. I was afraid this was going to happen," he says sharply and on edge.

A flash of cold sweat coats my body as the fear begins to sink in. My heart is beating rapidly, and I feel a panic attack developing. Darren must have sensed my distress and touches my shoulder. I look up at him with terror in my eyes. I'm not ready for this. It's too soon. I only learned about my father recently! And now the head of the council is here to see me?!

Without warning, Darren wraps his arms around me and hugs my body tightly against his. "I won't let anything happen to you. Just stay close to me, okay?" His body is stiff, and his muscles are tense under my touch. Why do I get the feeling that he's just as nervous as I am?

I shake my head and felt like I want to stay in his arms for a little longer. He pulls away too quick, making me lean forward a little from the momentum. "Quickly get dressed. You don't want to keep the head waiting," he warns.

Just as my fingers touch the fabric of my dress, I pause to look up at him, "I thought my dad was the head of the council?"

Darren stopped at the door. "He was. Someone is taking your father's place until the heir is found. Or in this case, until you make a choice. Since your father was the last one to be in the seat, only his kin can take over. No one can have the head chair officially until 21 years after the previous holder's death. It's a lot to explain Elizabeth, so I suggest you hurry and get dressed." He glances over his shoulder at me. The warning sends chills down my spine.

Looking down at the navy-blue material, I let out a heavy sigh. My head hangs back, and I stare at the ceiling for a moment before closing my eyes. "Mom, what did I get myself into?"

Once I'm in my dress, I ran a brush through my hair, smoothing it out as best as I can. If I had more time, I would put makeup on. I wore the same heels from the other night and quickly exited my room. As I walk down the hallway, I hear two male voices grow louder from the front door.

At the top of the steps, I look down at Darren, talking to a tall man wearing a grey suit and blue tie. His black hair is slick back, and he stands up straight. When he hears my heels clicking on the tile floor, he stops talking to Darren and turns to look in my direction.

"Well, here she is. The rumors don't do you justice," the stranger smiles and grabs my hand as soon as I am in reach. He kisses my hand longer than he needs to, making my skin crawl.

"Miss. Elizabeth. This is Master Lorcan Barclay, head of the vampire council," Darren introduces.

Lorcan finally lets go of my hand and smiles widely, his fangs poking out as he did. "Thank you, Darren, for that introduction. How about we sit to get to know each other, hm?"

Lorcan wraps his arm around mine, keeping a steel grip on me. I'm going to keep an eye on his movements and his fangs. Lorcan is too friendly, in my opinion, but then again, who am I to judge how a vampire should act.

We stroll together with our arms linked to the back of the manor where the gardens are. Lorcan pulls out my chair for me at the same table Amy and I had breakfast previously. His blue eyes sparkle in the afternoon sun as he boasts about his success in businesses. I ignore him and attempt to keep my heart rate steady. I don't want him to know how terrified I am. Soon, Darren arrived at my rescue with a tray of hot tea.

"So, Elizabeth, how does it feel having such a large home by yourself?" Lorcan asks.

I didn't answer Lorcan at first and just sip my tea. "It took some getting used to, but I like it."

I choose to take my time answering his questions. I wouldn't want to say anything stupid or insult him.

"Yes, well, Edmund liked to live modestly. I'm so sorry about his passing, he was a dear friend of mine and a great leader. To think he broke the sacred rule, though, but that is neither here or there," Lorcan smiles with a small hum and takes a sip from his cup.

His comment doesn't sit well with me and neither with Darren. I can hear his breathing get uneven as he stands behind my chair. "As lovely as this meeting is, may I ask why the visit?"

My question might have been disrespectful, but this man is in my territory now, and it was only right that I knew why.

Lorcan grins, finishing his sip of tea before wiping his mouth with his napkin. "Very direct. I like that. To see you, of course. There were many rumors of Edmund having a child for years, and it just so happened that a colleague of mine saw you drive up this way to Edmund's old estate. Naturally, I grew curious. There was nothing more I wanted to do than to meet the bastard child of Edmund," he sneers.

The fear that I had turned into a flame of anger, twisting in knots within the pit of my soul. I glare at him with as much intensity that I could muster to try and match him. "If this visit has anything to do about the manor, I haven't decided what I wanted to do yet. Furthermore, I might not even take part in or even look into the direction of my father's business with the vampire council," I state evenly, not sure what games Lorcan is trying to play here. I want him to know I am fully aware of what and who my father is.

His smile grew from ear to ear to the point that I thought his face might break. "Oh, my dear, I wasn't even worried about that. Besides, you only have a limited amount of time anyway, so I wouldn't worry about it," he chuckles and gets up from his chair.

"Wait, limited time for what?" I ask, standing up as well.

Lorcan ignores my questions and adjusts his tie. "I will be having a party in your honor this Saturday. It's not every day the heir of our once fearless leader resurfaces. Human or not."

The way he says 'human' makes me believe that he is enjoying this too much. A small part of me wants to tell him where to take his party and shove it, but I'm in no position to decline.

Smiling as much as I can muster, I nod my head. "Well, I look forward to your party."

Lorcan laughs and clasps his hands together, returning to the way I initially met him. "Excellent! Just let me know if there is anything I can help with. I'm here if you need me." His attention turns back to Darren, and with a small nod, Darren escorts Lorcan towards the patio door.

"Allow me to walk you out," Darren responds automatically.

I follow behind them at a distance back inside the manor. My arms cross over my chest as I stand by the staircase, watching Darren open the door. Lorcan grabs his coat and leaves without saying anything else to us. I watch Darren move to the window to make sure Lorcan is gone. When the coast is clear, he turns to look at me, and the stress in my shoulders evaporates into the air. "What was the point of all of this? Couldn't he call like everyone else?" I huff.

Darren stays silent as I rant on.

"Well, I'm not going. That man is not worth my time," I state stubbornly.

Darren rubs the bridge of his nose and looking at his watch. "Elizabeth, it would be unwise to decline the offer. Lorcan is a powerful man and head of the vampire council. You are in no position to decline. Especially since news of your existence is spreading like wildfire."

"It's obvious he doesn't like the fact I'm human or the fact I'm next in line. Why would he come all the way out here to see me? Something doesn't make sense," I ponder. Did he come out all this way to see if I am here?

"Perhaps he was curious. However, a part of me believes he wants to embarrass you at the part. You weren't brought up in the culture that vampires were, so you wouldn't know the etiquettes. He's essentially sabotaging your chance of taking the chair from him and your image to the vampire race," Darren mumbles softly and paces slowly, speaking what came to mind.

Well, this is great. I'm starting to think coming to this manor was the start of my death sentence. Once one obstacle was over, around the corner is another.

Finally, Darren stopped pacing and turns to me, "I would advise you to get well-rested. We will start training tomorrow morning in preparation for the party." I didn't get a chance to say a word as Darren calls for Reginald. "Reginald!"

The poor, old man wanders out of the kitchen,

holding his glasses in one hand and a white handkerchief in the other. He stuffs the cloth into his jacket pocket and put his glasses on.

"Prepare the ballroom for tomorrow morning," Darren orders.

"Right away," Reginald agrees. He wastes no time to hurry down the hallway and out of sight.

"Wait! Don't I get a say so in this?" I demand.

Darren stops walking away and looks over his shoulder at me. "You're in no position to get a say so. If you decline the offer, you will be ridiculed. If you show up not knowing anything about your vampire heritage, you will be giving exactly what Lorcan wants. Failure."

Slowly he comes towards me. My eyes wander up to his and latch on. He reaches out and pushes a few strands of hair from my cheek, gently brushing his fingertips against my skin.

"I refuse to let you fail. To be the laughingstock of the court. I promised you, no matter what, I would be here to protect you." He spoke softly and calmly compared to before. My heart flutters, and I take a step back. Darren was telling the truth. I absolutely was in no position to decline or show up like some uncultured swine. It was bad enough that I was going to be the center of unwanted attention.

"I guess I should get some rest then," I commented and quickly turned from his gaze and walks away. I rush back to my room and shut the door behind me.

My heart is drumming in my chest, and the blood

rushes to my head, making my cheeks flush. This is all starting to get to me. Only a few days ago, I packed up my mother's house and discovered that I actually had a father. He left me with a manor and now a legacy I really want nothing to do with.

When I'm finally calm, I stare out my window and wonder if mom was watching. Can you see me, mom? The torture I am in? I wonder what the difference would have been if I received my father's will four years ago. Would I be in the same situation as now? Or would I be even more in trouble?

Eventually, I change out of the dress Darren gave me and slipped into my black leggings and a white shirt. I stare out the window for a while, trying to decide if running away would be a better option.

There is a soft knock on my door, but I bluntly ignore it. I am in no mood to get a lecture from Darren at this moment.

"Lizzy? Are you awake?" Amy's soft voice fills my quiet room. When I refuse to answer, she walks in carrying a silver tray of sandwiches, chips, and soda. "I figured you were hungry and maybe wanted to have a girl's night," she smiles.

I feel like ever since the whole finding out everyone is a vampire thing, she is distant and careful around me. I guess I wouldn't blame her. If you kept a secret like that from your best friend for over four years, you would be distant as well. Turning to face her, I smile. I sit down on the bed and tap the seat next to me. "You don't have to act differently towards me. Just treat me like you did when we were in school. You're my friend first and whatever you are to me second," I grin, trying to repeat the same words she once told me.

Amy chuckles. "Good. I thought you were still mad when you didn't answer the door."

"No, no. I thought you were Darren at the door. He's making me take this vampire bootcamp tomorrow," I say, rolling my eyes.

"I heard. It won't be so bad. Darren is an excellent teacher." She grinned mischievously.

I rolled my eyes again and threw a chip at her. I wasn't about to open that can of worms.

"How is everything else?" She questions.

I know what she was referring to. I barely talk about my mother since the whole vampire fiasco. To be honest, I try really hard to block her death out. "I got an email yesterday that the house sold, and the lawyer will see that the money goes to the realtor fees and mom's medical bills. There will be a little left to pay, but not much."

Amy nods her head and eats a chip. "And how do you feel?"

I sighed and laid back on my pillow, staring up at the ceiling. "I miss her, especially now, with all of this going on. I wish she were here to tell me what to do. I feel so conflicted and angry because she never told me anything about my dad. When I asked, she told me he walked out, and that was the end of it. Did she even know he was a vampire?"

Amy shrugs her shoulders. "Your father didn't talk

about his personal life too much. All I know was the day your father telling us about you. That's all I can remember."

I wonder if mom knew anything about him. If she truly understood that he was a vampire and that could be the reason why she hid the will. Or, maybe she really didn't know that he was a vampire and she was trying to protect her only daughter.

"Hey, don't get so gloomy. Let's watch a movie and relax. You'll need it for all the training tomorrow," Amy kids.

I fish for the remote on my nightstand with a smile. As I flip through the millions of channels, Amy snuggles up next to me with our snacks.

"You know Lizzy, no matter what choice you make. I will always be here for you," Amy whispers quietly.

"Thanks, Amy. It's good to know that, no matter what, I'll still have a friend after all of this."

TEN

"Again!"

"Darren. I'm exhausted! We've been at this for hours!"

My feet start to protest after the third hour of dancing. I am still salty by the rude wakeup call Darren gave me this morning. He couldn't wait a few hours after sunrise to wake me up. No. He had to throw open the curtains, so the bright sun shines in my face. I'm pretty sure I hissed at him in retaliation. Darren was unphased and practically dragged me out of bed. Meanwhile, Amy snoozed away in the comfortable bed.

"We will stop at lunchtime for a break when you master the waltz," he commands.

I groan and run my hands over my sweaty face. The stray hairs are sticking to my cheeks, making me undo my ponytail and redo it over and over.

Darren is unusually bossy and persistent today. It makes me wonder if he is worried that I am going to embarrass him instead of myself.

"Let's go, Elizabeth," he barks.

I peel myself up off the floor and walk up to him, wanting to step on his shiny shoes in objection.

"If you got the rest, I told you to get you wouldn't be so tired. Instead, you stayed up all night watching horror films with Amaryllis," he taunts.

Even though he's right, I hated him at this moment. My face turns red as I place my hand on his shoulder and my other hand in his.

"Let's hurry up and get this done," I growl.

Darren grins, seeing how he is able to get under my skin. Reginald is standing by a stereo and presses play when Darren gives the signal. As we moved across the ballroom, our feet didn't miss a beat. Darren twirls me across the room, and I look up at the decorated ceiling. I wasn't surprised that the ballroom is beautiful. Everything in the manor is clean and furnished to the full extent.

The windows are tall and allow a lot of light into the small space. The marble floors shine as if they were just polished, and a small chandelier hangs above us, sending low rainbow light through the crystals on the wall. It is easy to tell that Reginald and Darren took outstanding care of this manor. I stop moving the moment my feet hit something hard. I stumble and quickly look down to see that I stepped on Darren's foot by mistake. He didn't flinch and just stares at me with annoyance.

"I'm sorry," I clear my throat.

Darren sighs, "Elizabeth, you need to concentrate.

How are you going to learn the dance if you keep spacing out?"

He's getting more and more annoyed with me as I shrugged. I didn't want to go to this party in the first place, but I need to go. I want to show Lorcan that I am more than just a human in his eyes.

"I don't know why I am taking the time to learn this dance anyway. I'm not taking over the council seat," I retorted.

Darren gave me a look. I wasn't sure if he is relieved or hurt. His face breaks into a smile and shrugs. "It's your choice. If it were me, I would do everything in my power to try and walk away. However, in the harsh reality of it all, each decision will have a consequence. Elizabeth, I am not here to persuade you otherwise. I am merely here to protect you. If you want to decline the position, then you need to make that clear at the party. All of the council members will be there, and if you want them to take you seriously, then I suggest we take it from the top and pay attention," he orders.

This is a losing battle. At this point, the only thing I can do now is to follow Darren's lead. Reginald presses play again, and our bodies begin to move. I focus as hard as I can on the steps, counting the movements in my head as we glide across the floor. I'm improving, but the thought of me dancing in front of complete strangers is nerve-wracking.

"Good, now keep up," Darren instructs.

The music starts to gradually increase to a faster pace, and Darren spins me around in time with the music. The further we get through the song, I begin to worry because we didn't get this far in the step explanation as we twirl one last time. I held onto his hand and trip over my foot.

Darren breaks my fall by catching me as I land softly on top of him. I look at him and want to curl up in a hole from embarrassment. "Oh, geez, I'm so sorry!" I gush.

He chuckles and reaches out to push a sweaty strand of hair from my face. I am confident he can feel my heartbeat through my chest. I went to look away, but he captures my chin with his thumb and turns my head back to him.

"You are doing exceptionally well," he says softly with hooded eyes as his face leans closer to mine.

"I beg your pardon, but lunch will be served momentarily," Reginald calls out.

The moment Darren and I were just sharing quickly dissolved as he got up and brought me to my feet. He brushes off his black pants and his white V-neck shirt.

"Yes, we will pick this up after lunch," he says, clearing his throat.

When he leaves the room, I stand there dumbfounded. Was Darren going to kiss me? The idea seems to shake me slightly because he's always so proper and focused. When we are alone, he shows more of his softer side and more relaxed.

After enough time passed, I walk out of the ballroom and trail after the sounds of plates and silverware to the dining room. The only time I walked into this room was when I first came to the manor. The long, dark, cherry oak table matched the chairs and shined in the low light.

Reginald and Amy were putting food on the table, and Darren is nowhere to be found. I touch one of the chairs and pull it out, so I could sit. The tops of my thighs are throbbing from all the dancing and practically sang to me the moment I can sit down. I feel like this basic training is a legalized form of torture for the out of shape soul.

Amy places sandwiches and veggies on the table, along with different fruits. My mouth is watering, looking at the delicious morsels, and I reach for a finger sandwich. Just as my fingers touch the soft, spongey bread, a hand came down hard on my skin, shocking me from my trance. I wave the sting from my skin and look up at Darren, who is hovering over me.

"Why did you do that?" I scowl, irritated that he is keeping me from my food.

"A vampire aristocrat doesn't simply reach out like some savage. We may be monsters, but we are more civilized than that," he scolds.

I frowned and said nothing as I slumped back in my seat. Darren is quick to lightly smack me in the back of the head, causing me to sit up again. "This is your next lesson. Etiquette," he states.

I'm a little confused and want to groan. I didn't know vampires keep up with manners in the first place.

"First, you must always sit up straight, don't slouch or lean on your elbows. A proper posture is important as it represents your upbringing," Darren instructs.

My eyes roll to the back of my head as I sit up straight and gently lay my hands on my lap. I notice Amy as she sits across from me, mimicking the actions. I'm not sure if she is being helpful or trying to be funny.

"Now, when you drink from your glass, you must do so quietly. Don't slurp," Darren continues.

"Do vampires ever eat food? I mean, they drink blood and stuff, right?" I ask in defiance. I've seen Amy eat regular food all the time, but the more I thought of it, it was always in small portions.

Amy slumps over now and rests her elbow on the table, propping her head up with her hand, proving my hypothesis that she is just mocking. Darren is pouring a cup of hot tea and sighs at my question.

"All animals and mammals adapt to survive. Vampires are no exception. Humans and vampires used to live in unity for hundreds of years. Vampires fed off the blood of animals mostly. They only fed on humans who were dying or sentenced to death. It was a peace treaty of sorts," he explains. "However, because of the war and with the human's uprising against vampires, we went into hiding. Thus, having to adapt. Without human blood, we had to rely on animals."

Reginald clears his throat, causing Amy and me to jump. We completely forgot he's still in the room because he is quiet. He smiles, seeing our reaction and pours himself some tea.

"To be honest, it was more of a way to make sure

we were fed. The humans feared us to the point where they would offer the convicted or the sick to please us. The blood was given to us as a way to keep us in check."

The way Reginald looks up at me sends chills race up my spine, making the hair of my arms stand up.

"Before your father took over the vampire court, there was a man named Claudius. He treated both races as if they were just his subjects, and he was the king. He was cruel and killed for fun. It was him that discovered that vampires can increase their power by the amount of human blood consumed. Claudius started a war where countless humans and vampires were slaughtered. He wanted vampires to be the supreme being. It was your father that stopped the war by killing Claudius. When the war was over, the remaining council members named your father the leader, not because he was one of the Ornigem, but because of his act of peace between the two species," he pauses to sip his tea.

Amy looks bored as she traces circles into the wooden table as if she heard this story thousands of times before. Darren and I are fixed on Reginald as he sits at the head of the table. The many lines in his skin move with his motions as he puts his teacup down.

"How old are you, Reginald?" I blurt without thinking. Instantly I get embarrassed as I wave my hand for him to dismiss my comment. "Sorry, that was rude of me. Just ignore me."

Reginald chuckles with a smile. "It's no trouble,

Miss. I'm about 400 years old. I was dying from sickness and turned into a vampire at the start of the war. I am still alive, thanks to your father. When he took over the council, all the vampires went into hiding, no longer allowed to consume human blood or be involved with humans. He was trying to protect both species," he sighed.

The story about my father's heroic nature surprises me. He put himself out there to protect humans and vampires by going up against one of his own. And in the end, it was his own rules that killed him. I wanted to ask Reginald more questions, but Darren beat me to the punch.

"Well, I guess that covers our history lesson for the day. Thank you, Reginald. We can walk in the sun and don't have to rely on human blood as much. However, some vampires still believe in Claudius' teachings, and kill humans for fun, draining their victims like it's a sport. We adapted to survive, not to take over." He describes.

Darren looks at his pocket watch. The day is slowly slipping into the early evening, and there is still so much to do.

"Speaking of food. I must apologize in advance for the lunch preparation. The steaks I had prepared for today were too tough to cook. Someone sucked them dry and completely forgot their manners." Darren glares at Amy as he arches an eyebrow in annoyance.

Amy gasps and places a delicate hand over her heart, acting as if she was offended. However, the smile she wore told a different story. "Me?! Why I never! But, if I can be frank, the cut of steak you got wasn't even that good. I prefer a juicy Ribeye." She snorts.

For the next few hours, Darren teaches me proper food etiquette and introductions. I understood most of the protocol, but the dancing is not working out.

By dinner time, my legs were on fire, and I couldn't move. I was lying on the waxed floor of the ballroom staring at the ceiling. My back feels sticky with sweat making my shirt cling to me. I'm fighting the urge to pass out as I think again about what Lorcan said, how it was only a matter of time. Time for what? It bothers me a little, not knowing what he meant. Did it have something to do about the council position? Or was it something else?

My eyes trace over the deep gold designs against the burgundy ceiling. The large chandelier stands still as the setting sun dips below the tree line. The once rainbow reflections are now dim and vanishing. The fake candles within the chandelier flicker on, bringing the room into a warm light. I often forget how beautiful the manor truly is.

"Is everything okay?"

I look up to see Darren standing over me with two water bottles in his hands. Carefully I sit up and could feel every muscle scream, begging me to not move. "I'm fine," I lie. Besides the physical exhaustion, I'm still worried about Lorcan.

Darren scowls at me and sits down beside me. He hands me a water bottle, which I instantly open to guzzle down the precious liquid. Once my insides are cold and happy, Darren stares at me, not convinced by my words.

"You don't seem fine. What troubles you?" He persists.

This is going to be another losing battle. He is going to bother me until I told him what is on my mind. I sip my water and spread my hands out in front of me to stretch. "I was thinking about what Lorcan said. It bothers me," I say reluctantly.

Darren looks at the large window in front of us. The tall evergreen trees sway gently in silence. "Before you take over your father's place, you have to be a vampire. No human can take the seat," he says.

"Well, that shouldn't be an issue, right? Don't you have to just bite?" I shrug. I must be insane. I'm talking as if I ultimately agree to the idea of being turned into a bloodthirsty monster to uphold my dear old dads' legacy. What am I thinking?

Darren chuckles, "How much television did you watch as a child? A bite isn't enough to change someone. Did you not pay attention the last time we went over this?" He pauses to take a sip of his water. It sounds like Darren is trying to be irritated, but his tired voice wouldn't let him.

"There is an exchange of blood and a blood ritual that needs to be performed to transform a human into a vampire. However, in your case, it's more complicated. Since your bloodline is that of the Orinegem, there is a different ritual. The ritual must be done by a pureblood from the Ornigem bloodline before your twenty-first birthday. The year twenty-one is a pinnacle year for our race. It's a ceremonial moment where the vampire has reached maturity. It was also when the first vampire was created, and it must be done under the red moon, which only happens every couple of years," he emphasizes.

I blink and think hard about what he said. "My twenty-first birthday is on June twenty-first. This is all too weird." I whisper.

"And the red moon will appear on that same night," he responds.

Which meant I have about a month to decide if this was the life I want. If I don't take the position, then the manor will be gone, and Lorcan will have full rights to the council.

"So, time is literally running out. My birthday is less than a month away," I groan, running my hands over my wet face.

As I try to wrap my brain around everything, Darren sits there quietly. "What should I do?" I ask him. Darren has been a big, more annoying, help so far through this whole vampire process, and I'm hoping he will continue to help me.

"Again, Elizabeth, I can't tell you what to do. This is ultimately your choice. The only thing I can do for you is to support whatever choice you make. If you choose to stay or if you choose to go. I am your servant. I am merely here to serve and support. However, I would be wary of your choice. If you choose this path and become a vampire, I am unsure of the dangerous future that lies ahead."

For some reason, I didn't like the way he said that. Hearing him say he was my servant makes my stomach curdle. I wasn't raised in the world of parties and servants, it's natural that I felt uncomfortable. Sure, I haven't known Darren or Reginald as long as I did, Amy. However, I never thought of them as low-class servants. To me, they are caretakers and maybe even friends in my eyes.

I only nodded at his words and didn't want to think any more of the situation. My only options are to either be human and be in danger or become a vampire, take over my father's place and be in danger. I wasn't left with a backup plan. My silence seemed to bother Darren as he stood up and shifted from one foot to the other.

"Let's stop for today and resume tomorrow. Get some rest," he says abruptly.

I feel almost defeated. The fate of my mortality is resting on my shoulders, and everything around me is crumbling. "Sleep sounds good right now," I stretch. My muscles protest with every step towards my bedroom. Each step I take feels like my feet were going to fall off.

The moment I lay my head down on my plush pillow, I could feel my body start to drift. Too many things happened today, and it's only the beginning. There is so much more that needs to be learned before this party. I only hope that I can keep up.

I feel so jittery like my mind is running, but my body stands still. My brain circles back to earlier today when I fell on top of Darren and how close our faces were. I could imagine his crystal eyes staring into mine, and` I felt stronger with all my worries far behind me. Throughout the training process and party preparation, the only thing I hoped for was that Darren would stay close to me. When I'm with him, he brings out the confidence in me. Soon my eyes slowly closed, and for a moment, my fears and Darren's face slipped into away.

ELEVEN

The past few days felt like a blur. Darren was very determined to make sure I knew every proper vampire etiquette. I feel like I'm cramming for a big test at the end of the semester. I did enough late sleepless nights, and it's starting to get old. No matter how distracted I was, the undeniable fear of being in a room full of dangerous vampires still haunt the back of my brain.

Amy is doing a great job of keeping me distracted, so my mind didn't wander. We argue playfully on different dress ideas and decide on a slim, black, floor-length dress with half sleeves and a plunging neckline. I usually would never wear anything like this, but Amy is insistent.

I have to admit, once I put on the dress, I look very regal in my new outfit. However, vampire or not, the fear of being judged is always something I struggle with. I had issues with judgment ever since I was a kid. My mom worked all the time and was hardly at home. She barely came to parent-teacher conferences or any school programs. The other kids knew I didn't have a father around, and it never stopped them from teasing me with their judgmental filled eyes.

Gently I place a hand on my bare neck as Amy stood behind me, curling my hair. The reflection of my face is foreign to me. I'm wearing more makeup than usual, and my long hair is pulled into the tightest French twist ever. Amy made sure to pull hard enough to flatten the bags under my eyes. If that wasn't over the top, the dress, she made me wear feel vulnerable and beautiful all at once. The soft black velvet fabric is smooth under my fingertips, and my entire neck area is exposed with nothing to protect it.

"Don't you think this is a bit much?" I ask, looking at her reflection through the mirror.

I watch her through the reflection, give my dress a once over, and scan my face. I smile to myself, little remembering the conversation with Darren the day before. I made a comment about how horrible it was to not be able to eat garlic. He was quick to correct me that during the time where vampires did their vanishing act, they let a rumor mingle that garlic was poisonous to their race and didn't have a reflection. It was a way to make sure the humans didn't turn on their own kind. All of it was laughable.

"Why do you think that? I think you look gorgeous!" Amy grins.

I'm not worried if I look good or not. I'm more concerned about the fact that my neck is completely exposed, and I'll be in a room full of vampires.

"I'm worried that I look like a walking buffet," I joke, pointing at my neck.

Amy bursts into laughter and gently places her hands on my shoulders. "You have nothing to worry about. No one would dare touch you. You're completely safe," she reassures.

I nod, knowing that Amy was right. As long as Darren and Amy are by my side, I won't be alone. They will protect me.

Once the finishing touches are done, I swear I'm ready for a movie premiere. Amy is looking lovely in her pink cocktail dress and makeup that complemented the bright, electric blonde hair she sported.

"Why didn't you wear one of your fancy dresses?" I ask while trying to stand in these hell heels Amy gave me.

Amy tucks a piece of her blonde bangs out of her face and grimaces. "The lower-class vampires aren't allowed to upstage the purebloods and aristocrats. Some of us who were changed are the lowest on the chain. I'm just lucky to be alive," she explains.

The idea of a strict social class like that wasn't right, but there are things about being a vampire that I didn't know yet. What am I thinking?! I never agreed to anything. There I go again. Considering that I could somehow be mentally okay with running a vampire race, I can barely keep up on the oil in my car. I'm only going to this party to save face, and then I am going to walk away from all of it. I can't get wrapped up into something that I know nothing about. If my father wanted me to take over his position, then he would have stayed in our lives and told mom the truth. This isn't my problem.

I've made my choice.

After the party and Lorcan announces my title, I'm going to surrender it to him. As much of a problem solver I am, I can't get tangled up in this world. I'd hate to see Amy, Darren, and Reginald out of a home, but I'll make sure to give them something to live off of after the manor is sold.

"Hey, are you feeling okay?" Amy asks, staring at my face.

"I'm just nervous," I lie.

"You will be fine. We should get going," she smiles, patting my shoulder.

It hurt to see Amy smile with such excitement when I knew I was going to leave after today. I can't keep the manor going, and I don't know enough about the vampire world. It's all only going to blow up in my face. We finally make it down the steps in the toe pinching shoes that I was given. I secretly pray we wouldn't be at this party for long since my feet were already starting to hurt.

Darren is at the bottom of the staircase, pacing back and forth, waiting for us to hurry. He sees us and taps at his invisible watch.

"We mustn't be late. It's important that we-" He stops his guilt trip the moment he looked at us. I watch his eyes shift from Amy to me. The way he is looking at me made me squirm, like an ant under a magnifying glass. I'm getting self-conscious in the dress that Amy made me wear, thinking I might look ridiculous. I'm exposed since I usually don't dress like this. I am more of a comfy sweater and spandex legging type of girl, not fancy dresses and hundred dollar haircuts.

Amy steps away with a small smile as I glance down at my feet. When I'm brave enough to look up, I saw Darren still staring at me. It's starting to weird me out to the point that I want to turn around, go to my room and hide in my covers.

"Is there something wrong? Is there something on my face?" I timidly ask.

Darren finally snaps out of his trance and clears his throat. He tenderly grabs my hand and brings it to his lips. My hand trembles and the goosebumps form on my skin, which I'm sure he notices. I'm also sure my heart skipped a beat or two, maybe three, and yet, I didn't want the moment to end.

I feel a smile form on his lips, and he looks up at me. "You look beautiful," he says softly.

I'm stunned by his smile and nod my head in response. Darren lets go and clears his throat again. "We need to be on our way. We don't want to be late."

Just like that, whatever moment we were sharing is now gone. For a moment, I can hear Amy's voice in the back of my head, making jokes, but Amy stays silent next to me and follows Darren to the front door. Everything in my mind is muddled with the thought of Darren's soft lips on my hand.

No. There was no way that I am falling for Darren.

Not when he acts so cool one moment and then distant the next. On top of everything, I know there is more to Darren than I realize.

The car ride to our destination is silent. Darren drove as Amy, and I sit in the back seat. I watch the trees turn into a blur, the faster Darren drives. Within hours we arrive at the most enormous mansion I ever saw. The building could fit at least three of my father's manors. There are men dressed in suits assisting people into the building and taking the cars away. I begin to fidget and play with my hands, making small circular motions with my thumbs on my dress. The velvet brushing against my skin seems to soothe my nerves a little. The further we drive up the long driveway, the harder my blood pumps in my ears.

Amy pats my knee and offers me a reassuring smile. "You'll do fine," she smiles. Easy for her to say, she isn't the one on the menu.

When the car stops at the top, I feel like all eyes are on me as I step out. The servants bow their heads slightly as I ascend the marble stairs. Darren and Amy are right behind me as we walk into the foyer of the mansion. I'm not sure this is a party for my honor, it looks more like a gala for celebrities. The women are dressed in the most expensive yet beautiful dresses. Their necks are decorated with massive jewels, and the men are wearing designer tuxes. I feel like a fish out of water.

I walk by groups of vampires, and they give me a side glance before keeping on with their conversations.

Darren and Amy slowly walk by my side and guided me towards the ballroom. The moment I step into the room, it's like someone put a spotlight on me. Subconsciously I grab Darren's arm to try and stay calm. He tenses under my touch, but he rubs my hand and gently returns it down to my side.

"Remember. You are like royalty. Amy and I are nothing but your servants," Darren mutters in my ear, but I can hear the strain in his voice. All of us are on edge, and we all need to be on our guard.

I realize now that I can't physically lean on them. The two of them are going to be there for me, just at a distance. We didn't get far into the ballroom when Lorcan sees us. He finishes his conversation with another guest and quickly saunters over in our direction. He couldn't contain his excitement as he smiles broadly and kisses me lightly on each cheek.

"Elizabeth! So glad you can make it!"

"Thank you for the invite," I murmur softly.

I looked around and saw Amy already disappeared, but Darren is still behind me.

"Now that you're here, we can get this party started," he announces. Lorcan takes my hand and pulls me towards the staircase in the middle of the ballroom. The dark, brown wood shines in the bright lights and leads to a second floor with a white handrail decorated in lavish flowers. We walk up about five steps, and he grabs two glasses of champagne from a waiter. He hands me the drink and looks at the beautiful crowd before us.

"Ladies and gentlemen. Tonight is a joyous occasion. The heir of the Montgomery household has returned, and with that, the leader of the vampire court. Edmund's daughter will be taking over my position as head of the vampire court, thus restoring the royal bloodline is once again. Let us drink to her success and the to the future under a new ruler."

People smiled and clapped as his voice rang throughout the room. Some people looked at me and then whispered to those around them or sipped on their drinks. I didn't have a chance to tell Lorcan I didn't want the position. He was too fast and hurried down the steps to greet more guests.

I carefully climb down the steps, as best as I could, and downed my champagne in one gulp. I'm going to need all the liquid courage I can get at this moment.

Looking towards the buffet table, I see Darren talking to a young maid. She giggles and holds a silver platter out to offer him a pastry. He smiles back at her, and something inside of me snaps. I feel like I'm being possessed by an aggressive entity as I watch the maid begin to openly flirt with Darren. I don't like this. I don't like how close she was to him. He is supposed to make sure I don't get eaten alive. Instead, he is flirting with a young girl. My blood is boiling. I have no idea why I am feeling this way. Maybe I'm acting jealous, but there is absolutely nothing to be insecure about. Darren and I aren't a couple. There was nothing romantic going on between us. None of this should be bothering me. Not to mention, our relationship was strictly business. Right?

The imaginative anger I'm feeling clouds my judgment, and I forget my surroundings. For a fleeting moment, I didn't realize where I was. The people around me fade into the background, and I'm brought back to my senses by bumping into a wall.

"Ow," I groan.

"Are you okay?"

To my astonishment, the wall had a smooth-talking voice. I was horrified to see that it was a guest and no barrier at all. I haven't been at the party for ten minutes, and I'm already causing a scene.

"I'm so sorry. I didn't mean to bump into you," I stammer. When I finally get the courage to look at his face, it's hard to not stare. His hair is pale and compliments the dark, emerald eyes he owns. My eyes trail across the room, and it's only then that I notice how wonderful everyone looked. I guess all vampires need to look like movie stars.

The handsome stranger bows to me, and I took a step back as he reached for my hand. "I'm Peter. Peter Vaughn, my lady." Gently he places a kiss on the top of my hand.

"Nice to meet you. I'm ugh, Elizabeth."

He chuckles and tosses back his blonde bangs from his face. "We all know who are Milady."

Wow, now I'm stupid. Of course, everyone knew me. This is what I was afraid of, being under the microscope while everyone watches me struggle.

"Right. Sorry, I'm still new to all of this," I gesture

around us.

Peter is friendly, but I have to be careful with my opinion. The last time I thought a guy was nice, I was drugged, pulled into an alley and had my head cracked open like a cantaloupe.

"Do you care to dance?" He asks.

The idea of dancing causes instant nausea in my stomach, but I knew I couldn't turn him down. I already have angry glares that are being thrown my way; if I turn him down now, it will only make me look bad.

"Sure."

I do my best not to hesitate and follow his lead to the dancefloor. My chest tightens as I look around the room as calmly as I could to find an escape route. Even though I agreed to the dance, I am having second thoughts. Visions of me falling flat on my face start to flicker in my mind and not helping to ease my nerves. The waltz plays softly, and my body goes into autopilot. Peter smiles at me as he holds onto my waist tighter and twirls me around. The music surrounds us, and I glide across the floor like a trained dancer. The only difference was that I wasn't stepping on any toes this time compared to practice. Darren would be proud.

I look for Darren on the sidelines and find him right away. He is standing still, with his eyes fixated on Peter and me. His face is scrunched up in angry or frustrated by the way his eyebrows wrinkle on his forehead. It isn't like Darren could dance with me. He even told me that servants were seen and not heard at gatherings. So, what is the big deal? Then it hit me. Was he jealous? The way his stare intensified as Peter pulled me tighter to him said everything. The idea of Darren being slightly jealous causes a flutter in my chest. Or maybe that's because of the constant twirling around happening.

As the song slowly came to an end, I look up at my dance partner, who bows and lets me go. "You are an excellent dancer," he comments.

I give a small curtsy, or what I thought was one.

"Thanks, I had a great teacher," I grin. Inside I'm beaming. I manage to get through a dance that I was dreading, and no feet were hurt in the process.

We didn't get a chance to talk more as a high pitch scream from a woman came from somewhere in the ballroom. Everyone's head turns in the direction of the source. Men dressed in black hoods and different masks begin to tackle the party guests with silver blades.

I couldn't move from my spot as people around me panicked. They are running in all directions, and it seemed that someone had locked the doors. For vampires, I thought it is a little uncharacteristic for them to act like this. However, I quickly see why.

One of the guards try making a run towards an attacker, but a hooded man shoves his silver blade right into the guard's chest. I stood witness as the man turns into a cloud of dark-colored dust, leaving his suit to fall to the floor.

Panic ripples throughout my body as people begin

shouting and fighting off the attackers. Everything is in slow motion as I twist around to find Darren. I see him fighting off a masked man and my voice is stuck in my throat as I attempt to call out to him. When he is free from the attacker, he plunged the blade into the man's heart, turning him into dust.

"D-Daren," I cry and ran over to him. He holds me close for a second and pushed me away at an arm's length.

"You have to leave this area and hide. I will come to find you when it's all over," he says in a rush.

I can't fathom the thought of him fighting these dangerous people alone or worse, to be separated and unprotected by him.

"No. I'm not leaving without you," I stubbornly insist.

Darren huffs and grabs my hand. "You better keep up then."

Darren pulls me quickly behind him as we dodge through the crowd and towards an exit. We are a few feet away from the door, and I could practically taste freedom when a hand grabs my free arm and yanks me out of Darren's grasp.

"Elizabeth!" Darren shouts as he spins around.

My whole body shakes violently as a masked man presses a blade to my throat. "Don't take another step, or the princess dies," he threatens.

Darren stops in his tracks as he bares his fangs at my captor.

"Just think, no one would have to die if you never

came around, little miss. All the vampires who died tonight was because of you," he sneered.

"Stop it! Elizabeth don't listen to him!" Darren yells.

"It's true. Our master said it so. We have orders to preserve the rightful heir to the throne."

"Enough!" Darren snarls and lunges towards us.

Darren is faster than the attacker. When the man's grip was loose enough, Darren was able to pull me away and shove the man back.

"No, you don't!" The attacker laughs. He gains his balance and is quick to lift his blade to strike.

I stumble in my heels and fall to the ground as Darren fell to his knees and held up his arm to protect himself. He hisses in pain as the blade gets stuck. I watch in horror as smoke rises up from Darren's arm, melting away his skin. He takes his foot and pushes himself away from the masked man. Within seconds Darren pulls the blade from his arm and jumps to his feet, digging the knife into the chest of the cloaked figure.

They both stop moving, and I fear the worse, but Darren slowly steps away. The masked man smiles as he stares down at the blade in his chest. His body falls to the floor, and his eyes never stray from me. "He will rise and prevail," are his last words before turning to dust before my eyes.

I'm hyperventilating, and my whole body is shaking so hard that my teeth are chattering. My mind is blank, and I can't comprehend what the hell just happened. Is this the danger that Darren warned me about? I scrambled to my feet and my heels caught in the hem of my dress. Darren is quick to keep me standing me even though he was injured.

"We need to get out of here," he urges.

"You're hurt, and we need to find Amy," I whimper, trying to stop my hands from shaking.

At the sound of her name, she appears from the balcony doors leading from the outside.

"Sorry, I'm late. There was a mess in the courtyard that had to be cleaned up," Amy pants while wiping her bloody hands on her already stained dress.

"How many?" Darren asks.

"There were six, but two escaped," she sighs.

Darren nods and holds his injured arm against his body. A wave of guilt rushes over me as I watch the blood drip from his hand and onto the marble dance floor. The people around us start to shout in anger at the mess. Only the guards are the one who was slain, the other guests were left unharmed.

The shouting grew louder as Lorcan stood on the ballroom steps. He held his hands up to try and get the crowd to calm down.

"Please. Everyone is safe now. The attackers were chased off. The council will get to the bottom of this. And I promise you, as long as I am still the leader, I will see to it that justice is served."

We lock eyes, and his sneer of a smile causes my skin to crawl. Once Lorcan is done talking, the guests calm down, but some eyes still shift my way. They glare at me with so much hate and disapproval.

"We need to get out of here and get your wound cleaned," Amy says, reaching out for my arm.

"Wound?" I ask, while frantically patting my arms.

I don't feel any cuts or blood, and I even checked my head. I check my left leg, and wince, feeling the kneecap was a little tender. I must have bruised it when I fell. I agree that we should leave and walk with Amy out of the ballroom. Darren followed us back to the car in silence and slid into the driver's seat. Even with an injured arm, he insisted that he should still drive.

People slowly start to leave Lorcan's mansion and towards their own cars. I can still hear the screaming and smell the scent of burning flesh from the guards turning to dust. This was all a horrible nightmare, and the faster we put this behind us, the better.

TWELVE

The car ride back to the manor was awkward. Amy and Darren sat in the front in silence, while I sat in the back, resting my head up against the cold window. The silence is deafening, and at this point, I would have preferred the two of them arguing.

When we arrive home, Amy insisted on helping me, but I had to instruct her to get cleaned up. I couldn't stand seeing the blood on her, she looked like shew as from Carrie. Darren, on the other hand, vanished.

When I was alone, I staggered my way up to my room, limping slightly from my bruised kneecap. The warm water of the tub relaxed my tense muscles as my eyes closed shut. I took a deep breath and realized my whole body stopped shaking. The muscles in my upper arms and back were sore from the tremors. How long was I shaking for? I didn't know I was that scared, to begin with. Maybe I was in shock? I just have to keep telling myself that it's all over now and that I am safe. For now.

After my bath, I change into a black tank top and a pair of pink yoga pants. The night's events weigh heavy on my mind, and images of the incident kept replaying. Who were those people that attacked? And why did they want me dead? I don't even want to be part of the vampires. Lorcan seemed too calm about the situation, but something wasn't right. It was something in the way he looked at me right before we left.

Eventually, I find myself lost in thought through the long hallways of the manor. I stop in front of a picture of my father dressed in a civil war uniform. I touch the frame and can sort of understand why my father took off. This world is dangerous, and I keep telling myself I don't want to be a part of it, but something keeps telling me otherwise. Ever since I found his will, my whole life decided to take an unnecessary pit stop, and that reserved resentment towards my father started to resurface again.

My mind is starting to stress myself out, and I need some tea to get my brain to shut off. If I keep stressing, it will give me a headache. Besides, the hallway is too quiet, and it's starting to give me the creeps.

The rest of the manor is just as quiet. The only sound I hear is the sound of my bare feet sticking to the marble flooring and peeling off with each step I take. When I reach the bottom of the steps, I see the light filtering from under the kitchen door. I open the door slightly, and Darren is sitting by the Island trying to wrap his arm. Every time he tries wrapping gauze around his wound, he drops the roll and curses under his breath. When he reached down for the roll again, I quietly walk into the kitchen.

"Here, let me help," I say, pulling a chair close to him.

Darren sits there when I gently grab the gauze from his hands and start to wrap his wound. My eyes trail to his white shirt and stare at the blood splatter all over it. I feel terrible at the position I put Darren in. He told me to run, but I refused. Now he's hurt.

"Why didn't you escape when I told you to?" He asks.

Is he reading my mind? Is that a vampire thing too?

I power through and continue to wrap his arm, cutting the gauze. I reach for the tape, but Darren prevents me from finishing the job. His hand clasps over mine, his touch is so gentle compared to the deadly demeanor from before. My eyes met his, and I feel myself getting lost again. The fuzzy feeling started up in my head, making my heart thump loudly.

"I was worried." I finally answer.

Slowly he lets go of my hand to let me finish what I'm doing. "I was worried that you and Amy would die because of me. These men that attacked tonight came for me. I know this now. Yet, I keep telling myself that it wasn't the case. In the end, it didn't matter, you still got hurt because of me."

The tears are whelming in my eyes. I'm always the strong one in any situation, and this past week made me feel so helpless. It's frustrating.

After I tapped the end of the bandage, I looked at

Darren with a forced smile as a tear trickled down my face. "Darren, I'm so sorry you got hurt because of me." I sniffed.

I didn't get a chance to wipe away the tear because Darren quickly pulls me into a hug. "Elizabeth. You never have to apologize if I get hurt. I vowed to protect you with my life, and no matter what, I will always be there," he says softly in my hair.

This time I didn't pull away. I want to stay in Darren's arms for as long as forever. My heart wouldn't let up as I close my eyes and breathe in his warm scent. I gently lean back after a few minutes and look up at him. Our eyes never strayed away as he gently places a hand on my cheek. His thumb rubs my skin tenderly, causing small goosebumps to form on my arms.

"I never want to see you cry over me again. I don't want to be the cause of your sadness," he smiles. His fangs poking out from his mouth slightly, but this time it doesn't faze me. Not like the last time I saw them.

I can feel his energy slowly reach out to me. My body felt like a magnet, and no matter how hard I pull away, he kept bringing me back in. "You could never make me sad," I whisper.

Darren closes the space between us and presses his lips firmly against mine. His lips were soft and smooth, and the fuzzy feeling in my head starts to clear as I place my hand on top of the one he had on my cheek. My eyes close as the time comes to a standstill around us, and we are encased in our own protective bubble.

That bubble pops as someone clears their throat,

making us both jump at the same time. My eyes shoot open, and I quickly get up from my spot, almost knocking over the chair I'm sitting on. Amy smiles, standing in the doorway of the kitchen and crosses her arms over her chest before looking at me. "I came to see if you were okay, Lizzy," she says quietly.

She didn't say anything about the kissing, and I nod wiping my sweaty palms on my pants.

"I'm sorry I wasn't there to protect you. If I were there, neither of you would be hurt," Amy frowns.

"It's okay, Amy. Everyone is alive, and that's what matters," I smile, walking over to her to give her a reassuring hug.

Amy hugs me back. She rubs my arms gently, grinning at me. "I'm heading back to bed. Don't stay up too late," she teased with a wink.

Shaking my head, I watch her leave relieved that that was the extent of her teasing. Amy can be a lot worse. She once teased me for a whole month for breaking up with a guy at school because he chewed loudly.

When I see Amy was gone, I glance back over to Darren. My face blushes as the intimate moment we shared prances around in my head again. Darren just smiles at me and slowly stands up from his chair. "I think we should follow Amaryllis' example and go to bed. Tonight, has been eventful."

I agree with him. My feet hurt from the pinching in my shoes that. My plush bed is practically screaming for me to lay down. Our feet shuffle as we walk up the steps, each step bringing me closer to my salvation. When we reach the top of the steps that split to the East and West wing, Darren grabs my hand and gently places a kiss on the top.

"Elizabeth, no one can know about us outside the manor. No one in the community can know because to the public eye, I am nothing but a servant. I never thought in a hundred years I would feel like this about anyone. I had a one-track mind, and that was to fulfill my promise to your father. But now I have a new promise, and that is to keep you safe and happy, and I'm not about to let anyone take you away from me," he says quietly.

A pang of guilt hit my heart, and our happy moment faded away right before my eyes. Did Darren really think that I was going to stay in the manor? Or, maybe he had hope that I would stay.

"Darren. I don't know what I'm going to do. I feel so confused. A week ago, I was cleaning out my home, and now I'm part of this vampire legacy that I'm not so sure I want to be a part of. My life is in turmoil, and I don't have a grasp on anything anymore," I gush.

Darren only smiles at me and gently places a hand on my cheek, caressing it softly. "I told you that I would stay by your side and protect you no matter what choice you make. Don't worry yourself anymore and get some sleep," he says softly and kisses my forehead.

I stand there at the landing and watch him walk towards the very end of the hallway. He disappeared into a door past Amy's door. Once he vanished from sight, I frown, knowing that even though he smiled, I still felt a hint of sadness. I'm sure he wants me to keep the manor just as much as Amy did, but Lorcan knows I would be here. And what if there was another attack like tonight? Would they get hurt or worse killed? I can't let that happen.

My bedroom door creaks open, and I rub an eyelash from my eye as I turn on the light. Something stirred in my bed, and I practically jumped out the window from the surprise. Amy sits with her back up against the headboard of my bed with her arms and legs crossed.

"Well, well, well," she taunts with a smile.

"What the hell, Amy! You nearly scared me to death," I yell, placing a hand over my heart, feeling the rapid beating.

"Did my eyes deceive me? Or did I witness you and Darren sharing a passionate kiss?" She teases more.

I should have known our little interaction earlier in the kitchen was a façade. It was only a matter of time before Amy began the teasing. She moves over on the bed, so I have a spot next to her. I roll my eyes, slightly irritated and sit down, still trying to calm my racing heart. However, I felt the intense stare from Amy's eyes, and I knew if I didn't answer her questions, she would never let up.

"We kissed only once. It wasn't what you think it was," I say, looking at her with a small grin.

Amy squeals and jumps onto her knees on the bed, bouncing up and down in excitement. My body bounces with her movements until she stops and claps her hands together a couple of times.

"I knew this would happen one day! Finally, you have someone worthy of you. I know for a fact he chews with his mouth closed," she laughs.

"Amy!" I yell softly, grabbing my pillow to hit her with it. "First off, that was like three years ago, it's time to let it go. Secondly, I'm surprised that you didn't want to snatch him up. Were you waiting all this time to see this would happen?" I question. I'm starting to think all of the things that are happening to me are all purposely done.

The smile from Amy's face falters, and she sits back on the bed, returning her back to the headboard.

"To be honest, I wasn't expecting any of this to happen. When you told me you found the will, it was only a matter of time for everything to lead up to this moment. As much as I platonically love Darren, absolutely no. Darren is like an older, more annoying brother to me. I was rooting for the two of you since we came to the manor. Darren never ever opened himself up to anyone, but with you, he talks more and is more tolerable than normal. You two make a fine match." She nods as her smile returns to her face.

I bit my bottom lip gently, I thought about what she said, and I could see what she meant. The first day I came here, Darren was quiet and kept mostly to himself. He only gave short answers and ignored most of my questions. Since our bootcamp, he's opened up more, and I'm getting real solutions instead of half-assed ones. Perhaps, this is my destiny all along? Would mom approve of this situation?

"You know, since all of this started and for how confused I am, I'm starting to think that no matter what choice I make, it's always going to lead here," I say softly, drifting off into thought. "Now that I think of Amy, you never really dated anyone in school. You told me you were on regular dates but, now I'm wondering how true that was."

It was my turn to ask questions now. Even though I don't like bringing up the fact that Amy lied to me for four years. I think it's time that I learn who Amy really is and not the lies that she was feeding me from before.

Amy smiles sadly and letting her head drop a little, "Yeah, I went on a few, but that was only to fill the boredom. Most of the time, I was constantly keeping watch in case unsavory people tried snooping around."

"So, you never had anything serious?" I ask.

"When I was first turned, it was during the French Revolution. I was living in Paris and worked as a servant girl for this family. Little did I know, the family was vampire aristocrats that were part of the Second Estate. I wasn't the only human servant they had, but I was the clumsiest. The family had a son named Henri, and he used to torment me. He would give me the hardest jobs and would still find things for me to do. To his dismay, I would overcome every obstacle he gave me. After a while, he slowly stopped and became nicer to me, seeing that he couldn't break me." Amy takes a breath and looks down at her hands as she plays with the hem of my blanket.

"We fell in love and met in secret. Eventually, he told his family, and that did not go well at all. Things began to get violent during the revolution, and we were trying to flee. Someone grabbed ahold of Henri and killed him before the family by beheading him. He hadn't reached his twenty-first birthday and didn't reach vampiric maturity yet. I was beside myself, and the family blamed me for his death. As a punishment, they turned me so that I could live the rest of my days with the guilt of his passing.

When we found our new home, they were abusive to me and didn't stop until Master Edmund came for a visit. He saw how malnourished and weak I was and requested that I serve him instead of the family. They agreed, and to my surprise Master Edmund was nothing but kind to me. He told me what happened with Henri wasn't my fault, and I can't let things from my past keep me from going forward in the future. I had only one true love, and I don't think I can let myself go through all of that again. It's weird, I never told anyone this. Not even Darren." Amy says with a shrug.

I am speechless, and the only possible thing I could think of to do was reach out and place a hand on her shoulder, rubbing her pale skin with my thumb.

"This is what friends are for, and my father was right. You can't let your past stop your future. One day you'll be able to move on but do it at your own pace." I nod.

Amy snakes her arm around my waist and gives me a small side hug. It isn't as tight as her previous hugs, but I know she is hurting. I slide my arm around her waist in return and rest my head up against hers. We close our eyes for a moment, like we are meditating, and take a deep breath.

It was finally my turn to be there for her when she needed me and not the other way around. I'm glad that Amy opened up to me because now her healing process can begin. Even though this happened to her hundreds of years ago, it was never too late to heal.

THIRTEEN

A few days after the attack, I try to keep myself out of everyone's way. Darren respected the space I wanted and did his best to not bother me. My poor neglected station wagon sat in the gravel driveway with its trunk still full of what little property I owned. The boxes from school sat untouched, filled with clothing, posters, and my professional camera. Going to New York for Photography sounded like such a fun idea at the time, but now I'm only left with a box full of pictures from past assignments and a diploma that will never be framed.

I sit among the gardens using my camera to take up-close color photos of the roses. The morning sun shines lazily on the drops of dew on the rose petals. A monarch butterfly perches carefully on a leaf cleaning its face. I lift my camera up to snap the picture, but the sound of a female's voice causes the insect to fly away. I groan, looking up at Amy, rushing over to me on the ground.

"Lizzy! You need to get cleaned up and dressed," she demands.

I would have expected this sort of demand from Darren and not from her. I groan louder and lie down in the fresh grass as a form of defiance.

"Just five more minutes," I whine.

I forgot how good it feels to have a camera in my hand again to capture life's moments.

"I would love to give you more time, but I can't. You have a guest, and it's urgent," she insists.

I roll onto my back and slowly got up from the damp ground giving her a huff. Pieces of grass clung to my shirt as I wiped away the strands. Deep down inside, I hope that it wasn't Lorcan trying to apologize for what happened the other night.

This time I didn't have to wear a stuffy business suit like the last time I met Lorcan. Instead, I was able to wear something more comfortable, like my yellow sundress. It had a statement that said, 'yes, I'm dressed cute, but I'm also lazy at the same time.'

Walking down the stairs to the foyer, I start to become anxious about what was waiting for me. As if my life hasn't been eventful enough already.

Darren is talking to a tall man with short, dirty blonde hair. They talk briefly and turn to me as I step off the last step.

"William? This is a surprise?" I say in astonishment. Seeing my father's lawyer was the last thing I was expecting. A striking fear crept up into my chest as I look at Darren, hoping that William didn't discover the vampire secret.

William embraces me briefly and kisses me on both cheeks, any formality is entirely out the window. "I believe we have much to discuss," he smiles as a small fang poked out of his lip.

He links my arm with his and leads me towards the dining room where tea and snacks are waiting. "Something tells me this isn't about selling the manor, is it?" I ask, trying to hide the shock from my face. So, William is a vampire as well. To think you know someone.

William chuckles and pulls out a seat for me at the head of the table before seating himself. "I'm afraid so. Some things needed to be sorted out before I could come to you," he says softly.

It's weird. William has this warm demeanor compared to some of the other vampires I met so far. He has this persona about that makes him so inviting, but maybe it makes him dangerous at the same time.

"I was at Lorcan's party under the suspicion that he was up to something, and I was right. Normally, I would stay away from all vampire council functions for the simple fact I can't stand them. However, I wanted to see if he invited you and that it wasn't a ploy. I was pleasantly surprised you showed up and looked radiant," he grins.

"Why didn't you say hello?" I ask as I pour some tea for the both of us.

He takes a sip and sighs, "I would have, but I was undercover. The vampire council and I don't get along.

I didn't come here to catch up, Elizabeth. I came here to tell you that the attack at Lorcan's estate was staged by Lorcan. I managed to grab one of his henchmen and gave a convincing interrogation. Needless to say, he told me everything."

My stomach feels like it's doing backflips. I knew Lorcan was trouble the moment I met him. The fact that it is confirmed makes my dangerous situation more apparent. I see Darren out of the corner of my eye by the door. His body stiffens a little but relaxes when our eyes met.

"Lorcan is threated by you, Elizabeth. If you take over, then he will be removed from the court. I also have reason to believe that Lorcan killed your father. Edmund came to me shortly before his death to draft his will. When I asked him the specifics, he kept me in the dark. After his death, I began to question the council. Let's just say my accusations with the certain members of the council are what got me in trouble." He says with a smirk while taking a sip of tea.

"When you first stepped into my office, I couldn't stop thinking about how much you reminded me of your father. Well, maybe not as mischievous." He chuckles.

"Mischievous? From everything I've heard, he sounded like a boy scout," I shrug.

William laughs and sighs, sitting back in his seat. "We were a couple of hooligans back in the day. In the days before the great vampire war, we were young and couldn't sit still. Vampires were under strict rules, and we would rebel against the council by terrorizing them. We would let chickens loose in the chamber and chase after the young maids," he smiles.

Picturing a young William trying to gather chickens to let loose in a meeting made me laugh with him. After a bit, I see a glimpse of sadness wash over him. He stares at the wall in front of him, where a picture of a gazebo on a pond in soft pastel sits.

"I miss my dear friend. Up until the end, he only spoke of your mother and how much he loved the two of you. He wanted nothing more than to protect you." William says softly, bringing our happy feeling to a halt.

He slowly reaches into his pocket and pulls out a handkerchief. It looks old and fragile, with holes poking through the white fabric. Gently he takes the bundle of cloth and places it on the table, sliding it towards me. It is wrapped around something that looks heavy and makes a metallic dragging noise when pushed.

I stare at the lump for a moment and pull the cloth away to reveal a key. It is made of brass and looks like an old skeleton key.

"A key? What is this for?" I ask, perplexed.

"Right before your father died, he gave me that key to giving to you when the time was right. I vowed to your father that I would watch over you until you made your decision. He said the 'truth will be revealed when the key finds its home.'" He smiles.

I look closer at the key and touch the teeth thinking back to the box in my father's study. Maybe this key is for that box?

"When you make your decision Elizabeth, come visit me at my office. It will be fun to get better acquainted with my niece," he beams and slowly rises from his seat.

Hearing him call me his niece, it makes me feel a little at home. Even though the family I had is gone, I'm starting to discover a new family here for me. I smile and stand up too. "Should I start calling you, Uncle William?"

He flashes a bright smile at my teasing. "How about Uncle Will instead?" He chuckles.

William reaches out a hand to shake mine, but I walk right past it and wrap my arms around his waist, hugging him. It caught him by surprise. He grew rigid at first but slowly wrapped his arms around me, giving me a hearty hug.

After our embrace is over, I watch Darren escort William out of the dining room. The key feels heavy in my hand, and my palm itches with anticipation of what this key will unlock. I wait for a few minutes and hurry out of the dining room, down the hall, and into my father's study.

This key holds all the answers to the missing pieces of my life, and I need to find out the truth.

FOURTEEN

If my hunch is right, this key should unlock that box I found.

The study is in the same manner that I left it in. Papers were still stacked on the desk, books in the looming towers on the floor, and the curtains opened slightly to let just enough light into the darkroom.

The only thing absent from this room is a fine layer of dust, which I'm sure Reginald or Darren probably cleaned off.

Sitting back in the chair behind the desk, I stare at the key before opening the drawers. A tiny part of me wants to ignore everything that is going on and say, 'Not my problem,' but there is the urge to know exactly what happened the night my father disappeared. I open the drawer carefully and pull out the wooden box I found on my first day at the manor. The key fits perfectly, and like a well-oiled machine, it opens with a soft click.

I find a thick book that was is rough around the

edges. Pieces of paper are sticking out the sides, and the string holding the book together is tattered and brittle. The cover of the book is labeled with initials *"E.M."* in faded gold letters. I open the book gingerly to reveal yellowed pages with fading brown ink. They are journaling entries, all dating back as far back as the 1600s. After a few more page turns, I see the handwriting get progressively neater. My father kept a journal throughout his whole life. I notice some entries were smaller than others and stop randomly on a page to look at the date.

Nov. 21, 1701

"It's been another gruesome day out on the field. The humans are getting wiser to our weaknesses. William said it might be another few months before this town would be empty of humans. Veon will stop at nothing until all humans are dead or slaves. I'll never understand the man's way of thinking. Yes, they are the weaker species, but should it not be our responsibility as the stronger species, to protect those who could not?

The council made all executive decisions on ceasing all interactions with humans as per the head Veon. William was distraught when all capable vampires were forced into an unnecessary army. There was nothing we could do to stop this from happening.

One thing is certain. Veon needs to be stopped before things get worse. Too many human lives are being lost along with our own. When will it all end? When all humans are dead or enslaved? When all

*vampires are dead? I wish for the day when vampires
and humans could live in peace. No more hiding and
no more violence. To be able to have a family and
friends with no consequences. However, there might
never be a day like that. One can only dream."*

My father wanted nothing more than for everyone
to get along. In the end, it was his downfall. I page
further through the thick book and stop on an entry
that was a little more recent.

April 25, 1971.

*"Humans are strange and complicated. After
hundreds of years and after the horrific torture my kind
placed on the human race, you would think we learned
everything we could about them. They keep surprising
me.*

*Since my succession to the head of the council, I
kept the same rules that were in place from years ago.
No human relations at any cost. As society started to
evolve, our kind had to, as well. I wanted to make the
world a better place, but humans became greedy over
time and too fearful. After six centuries of moving
around, I believed my talents were best suited in
Virginia, where I can work in congress or some sort of
politics. It's like fate brought me to this small town on
purpose in some sadistic joke.*

*I saved a girl today. No, she was a beautiful, strong-
headed woman. She was dressed in colorful skirts and
flowers in her hair, shouting at my place of work for*

peace, love, and no more war. I was transfixed by her aura and stopped an officer from arresting her. She yelled at me, telling me how, 'the man was bringing her people down,' but I was too busy focusing on her beautiful freckles that dotted her nose. Debra Evans. Reluctant to accept my help at first but stopped resisting when she realized she would be jailed. As much as she wanted to fight me, she was quick to comply until she was safe. I never met someone so passionate about their fellow species, and I was enthralled.

William said I was going to hell for getting involved with a human. Oh, how much fun I'm going to have along the way."

Tears prick my eyes as I continue to turn the pages. I couldn't remember how many times I asked mom how she met my father. The answer was always the same, "I don't remember" or "It was so long ago." Now I had some closure and not very surprised that my mother was at a peace rally. It's almost romantic how they met.

The moment of nostalgia was short-lived when I stopped on an entry two months before my birthday.

April 25th, 1992

"I should have known it was all too good to be true. That my happiness was going to be short-lived. Debra will be having our child within a matter of months, and someone found out. I didn't have time to get things in

order. William was going to take my place in the council, so Debra and I could run away and raise Elizabeth without the fear of Veon's followers. I received a cryptic letter today at work with the ultrasound pictures I had in my briefcase. In order to protect my loved ones, I have to leave them. Debra didn't know about me, so they are safe for now. I was going to tell her before I proposed. How foolish could I be? I should have told her years ago, but I couldn't bear the thought of losing her. When did I become such a selfish man?

It kills me every time I look at her picture or of the ultrasound. To know that my whole life was taken away from me in a moment. The sounds of Debra's cries as I left, will forever haunt me. I only wish that one day, vampires can come from hiding so I can be reunited with my family once more."

The lump in my throat grew as I finish reading. The anger I once held for my absent father, slowly melted into sadness. My father only wanted humans and vampires to be able to coincide in society, to be able to live and work. Why was that such a crime? He loved us, and I can tell by his writing that he didn't want to leave.

The last written page of the journal was only four years old.

July 17, 2012.
"There is no more hiding now. Lorcan found where

I had sealed myself away and is forcing me to come out. I know it was him who blackmailed me all those years ago. If my suspicions are correct, I will be dead by sundown.

I lived my life with many regrets but loving and being loved by a human was not one of them. Debra was my salvation for the nightmares that plagued me. Elizabeth was the shining star to guide me in my conquest for peace among humans and vampires. If I die, I will die knowing that my family is safe.

To Elizabeth. If you are reading this, then it's clear that I am no longer of this world. I trust you've grown into a strong woman, just like your mother. By now, you've learned about your heritage and the role you play. No matter what choice you make, even in death, you have my full support, and I am proud of the person you've become. William, Reginald, Darren, and Amaryllis are there to help you along the way. I trust them with everything.

I hope one day you can forgive an old daydreamer for the foolish idea that I could live a life of bliss with no consequences. I will always love you and your mother. Until we meet.

-Your father, Edmund."

The tears continue to flow from my eyes as I close the journal. The wall I spent years building around my heart crumbled into a million pieces. My father loved me, and even in death, he is reaching out to me to make the right choice.

I will be damned if I let a bastard like Lorcan get away with ruining my family or any other family. I am going to take my father's place as the head of the vampire council. I will protect the human and vampire race as my father once did. My father was right, I did grow up as a strong woman like my mother and ten times more stubborn too. I just hope Lorcan is ready for it. My twenty-first birthday is less than a month away, and I don't have time to waste.

"Darren!" I shout. It only takes a second for him to come barreling into the room. For as graceful as he typically is, it's almost funny to see him stumble.

"What's wrong?" He says, panicking a little.

I stand from my seat and pick up my father's journal. I hold it in my hands as I look up at Darren. "Find Reginal and Amy. I think it's time we have a meeting with the vampire council," I smile.

Darren matches my smile and bows to me like he did on the first day we met. "As you wish, Milady."

FIFTEEN

"Yay! Oh, I knew this day would come!" Amy shrieks. I didn't get a chance to say anything as her body crashes into mine, and she smothers me in her vice grip hug.

"Thanks, Amy," I chuckle and pat her elbow since my arms are stuck at my sides.

When she finally let's go, I feel like I can breathe again. Reginald smiles and pours everyone a cup of tea, placing each cup at a spot on the dining room table.

"I realize now that I can't sit back and let Lorcan continue to be the leader. If he is there permanently, then human and vampire lives will be at risk. The evidence against him is too substantial to ignore," I say evenly. "Loran killed my father, tore my family apart, and every fiber of my being tells me that he was trying to kill me that night at his estate. He must be stopped and brought to justice."

Reginald nods with each of my words and sips his

tea quietly, "Spoken like a true leader. Those were the same words your father said when he rose against Veon."

"It will be dangerous, so Amaryllis and I will come with you," Darren replies.

"Then it's settled. We will leave tomorrow morning and tell the council that I will take over my father's place." I smile.

Everyone agrees as they mentally prepare themselves for what might happen tomorrow. Why couldn't I get some vampire powers ahead of time and predict the future? I highly doubt that that was possible, and to be honest, I'm not sure I would want to know. Even if I could.

Darren clears his throat to bring everyone's attention to him. "We cannot let our guard down, and we cannot accuse Lorcan of his treachery in front of the council members. It will be a sign of treason towards our kind. Remember, Lorcan is still the head until your coronation Elizabeth," he informs.

Great, I'm going to go through a whole public affair too? Why do vampires have to do flashy things? However, I understood where Darren was coming from. We can't make any rash judgment calls until I am officially in the head seat.

"Alright, then. We should probably get some rest before tomorrow's adventure," Darren sighs.

"Darren, heed my warning. You must take caution tomorrow. Lorcan is more powerful than you think. It won't take much for him to rally an army against you should something go wrong," Reginald warns.

Darren only nods and escorts me towards the staircase. Reginald stays behind to finish his tea as Amy skips off to her bedroom.

Sleep is the last thing on my mind right now, I was too quick to make plans to see the council that I forgot about the danger I would be in. Darren assures me that everything will be okay and kisses my head before going down the hallway. I stand there and stare out the window at the top of the steps trying to mentally prepare myself for tomorrow.

*

I am already awake by the time the sun rose and shined through my window. I didn't get any sleep from the night before. I wasn't too surprised because I always have a habit of tossing and turning when I was worried. In the end, I only had an hour of sleep.

Everyone is silent in the car. Darren drove while Amy sat in the front passenger seat. I sat in the back, staring out the window in a tired haze. The grey dress suit Darren made me wear is suffocating. The shoulder pads in my blazer make me feel stiff, and the hem of my wool skirt is causing the backside of my knees to sweat. I feel so uncomfortable to the point that I am prepared to jump out of the window.

My mind wanders, and I start to ask myself if mom was proud of my choice. Would she have been horrified that my father was a vampire? Or, maybe she wouldn't have cared? Perhaps she was finally at peace knowing that all her unanswered questions were brought to light? I know I am somewhat at peace. I will be more at peace once Lorcan was out of the picture. It is my turn now to continue my father's vision. Who knows, maybe I will be able to abolish the human-vampire law. This way, families will never have to be torn apart like mine was.

The long three-hour drive to the vampire council is tedious as the cities turned to trees and trees back into cities. No one talks the entire way, which makes the atmosphere more uncomfortable than my outfit. After the next patch of trees, there is a long black iron gate that had to be at least four hundred yards long, surrounded by tall fir trees.

Darren slowly pulled up to the gate entrance and pressed a little button. A gruff male voice comes through the speaker box in a language I never heard before. Darren responds softly in the same gibberish, and the gate began to open smoothly.

Once through the gate, my hands began to sweat as my skin became all prickly. I feel like someone was sending an electric current through my body, making my hair stand on end. The driveway is long, and I thought we would never reach the top of the hill. The large building at the top puts both Buckingham Palace and The White House to shame.

As I marvel at the structure, the car slowly came to a stop. Darren opens my car door, causing me to jump. "Are you ready?" He smiles while holding out his hand for me.

"As ready as I am going to be," I sigh and slowly slide my hand into his.

Once out of the car, we walk up the stone stairs. Darren is to my left, and Amy is standing on my right. We are greeted by an elderly man at the door and bows his head when we walk through the threshold.

I thought for sure we stepped into a museum. Large portraits of past leaders lined the walls along with maps and artifacts in glass cases. Old documents were laid flat and pinned to the wall with a protective cover on them. All of the papers were in languages that I didn't recognize.

The older butler follows us as we strolled down the hallway. When we finally came to a stop, he looks at us with hooded eyes. "The council is in the chamber room awaiting your arrival. Shall I bring you a chair or a refreshment?"

"That won't be necessary. We don't plan on staying long," I respond. My nerves are starting to bundle together in the pit of my stomach. If it weren't for Darren and Amy by my side, I know I would have passed out by now.

We are escorted to a large, dark, oak door with gold trimming. The doors slowly open, and I walk in first. The sound of my heels clicking against the floor is deafening in the silent room. Darren and Amy stay back as I stop in the center of the chamber.

There are five cabinet members of the vampire council. Lorcan sat in the middle, and two older men sit to the right of him and two older women to his left. All of their eyes are on me, and I feel the slight hint of judgment coming from their stares.

"Miss. Evans. What a lovely surprise. To what do we owe the pleasure of your presence?" Lorcan asks softly, adjusting his black robes.

The minute he said my name, I see it click within some of the other cabinet members. Their subjective looks change to excitement as they broke into small conversations. I take another brave step forward and look at all of the council members. I had to be careful, though, the moment I let my guard down could be the end of me.

"I, Elizabeth Evans, come before you today to discuss my place within the vampire council. Ever since I was a child, I wanted to know who my father was. I got to the point in my life where I gave up wondering. I thought it was best to know that my father simply left, and I came to terms with that. For years I had this anger and resentment towards him. When I discovered that I have this bloodline and this lineage to uphold, I instantly rejected it."

My voice fills the room, and it wasn't until I stop speaking that I realize my voice is echoing. The place remains silent, and it seems like everyone is holding their breaths. The smirk Lorcan has on his face made me want to slap it off.

"However, I also realized that I can't deny my heritage or deny the legacy my father left behind. I understand he was well respected by the community, and I hope, in turn, I also gain the same respect. I decided that I will be taking my father's place as your leader and head of the council."

The smile Lorcan was wearing slowly diminished to a grimace. The rest of the council members are elated. A few of them left their seats behind the long wooden table to shake my hand and bow their heads. I didn't catch any of their names as they hurry out the door to plan for a coronation and to spread the word. They were all talking so fast that I didn't catch all the words. One older woman is left behind near the table. Her jet-black hair is tightly wound on her head into a bun. I was sure if it is undone, her face would fall, and all her wrinkles would show her real age. She leans into Lorcan and whispers in his ear before giving me a sideways glance.

The hair on the back of my neck stood on end as I watch her leave through a side door, never speaking to me. Before I had a chance to wonder who that woman was, Lorcan appears before me.

"I guess congratulations are in order," he smiles but doesn't look very happy.

Darren slowly moves behind me as Amy stays in place. Lorcan's smile turns more sinister as he continues to speak. "Enjoy your small victory while you can. If you aren't a full-fledged vampire on your birthday, then you can't be the leader. Not to worry, though, I'll make sure that it will never happen." His eyes are fierce as they hold onto mine, and without saying anything else, he walks away.

The drive home is just as quiet as the trip to the vampire council. Darren said nothing after Lorcan walked away, and Amy only grabbed my arm in silence. When we arrive home, Amy didn't say anything to us and quickly went inside. She is acting strange, and it concerns me.

"Is Amy okay?" I ask.

Darren closes the front door behind us and sighs. "I'm sure she will be okay."

I stare at the stairs as Darren disappears towards the kitchen door. I follow my instincts and walk up the steps to the second floor, venturing towards Amy's room. I gently knock on her door and wait for her to answer, when she doesn't, I push it open with little force.

"Amy?" I call out.

There is some silence followed by light sniffling. Amy is sitting on a chair near one of her bedroom windows. Her room is decorated with a mixture of modern times and items from the Victorian era. I feel like I walked into an antique shop.

"You okay, Amy?" I ask as I walk closer.

Amy nods her head quickly and rubs her eyes. "Yeah, I'm fine. I just never thought I would ever see her again."

"Who?"

"The woman talking to Lorcan before we left. Her name is Camille Delacroix. She's my former mistress and Henri's mother. I never knew she was in the council. Seeing her for the first time after so long, I froze."

I reach for her shoulder and pat it gently before wrapping my arms around her shoulders, giving her an awkward hug. Amy was there for me when mom died, it was only natural that I would be here for her. Losing someone you love is hard, but the punishment that Amy was put through was pure torture.

"Amy. Do not give her the satisfaction of knowing that she still gets to you. Be strong. Show her how much you have grown as a person. She does not have control over you anymore. I'm sure Henri would tell you the same."

Her head rests against mine, and I can feel her breathing slow down. Soon I feel her arms wrap around my body, crushing me in her signature hug.

"Thank you, Lizzy. I really needed this," she whispers.

When I knew she was okay, I left her alone so she could paint her nails. She offered to do mine after our talk, but I want to find Darren so we can talk about our next step.

Darren wasn't in the kitchen or in the study when I search for him. I found him in the last place I would see him. He is standing on the patio looking out into the darkness of the trees that lined the yard. I gently shut the door behind me and walk towards his silhouette. I stand next to him in silence and take in the damp woods surrounding us. Darren and I are alone, and the adrenaline from standing in front of the council starts to drain from my body. My legs begin to shake slightly as Lorcan's words buzz around my head. "Darren, what needs to be done? What do we do next to make me a vampire?" I ask.

The moon was starting to rise, and stars began to dot the sky with their brilliance. He wraps my arm around his arm, stroking my hand and sit down on the stone steps that lead deeper into the gardens, the cold stones making goosebumps rise on my skin as soon as we sit down. Darren looks at me and then up at the sky.

"Humans require a vampire to conduct a blood ritual on the new moon. Rituals were banned because there was more mixed blood than pure-blooded vampires. The council ruled the rituals out because it was the start of the idea that humans and vampires shouldn't coexist. In your case, since you are from the Ornigem bloodline, no ordinary vampire can perform the ritual. It must be done by someone of that bloodline. Blood that powerful is the only way to completely take over the human inside of you."

I frown and look down at the roses as the wind rustled them, trying to take in all of his information.

"It makes things difficult for us because the next new moon is on your birthday, and there is only a handful of the Ornigem left," Darren sighs.

"So, our plan is simple then. Find a vampire with the Ornigem bloodline, convince them to change me, take over as the leader of the council and expose Lorcan for the snake he is," I say sarcastically happy.

Darren smiles and wraps his arm around me,

holding me tightly against him. "You need to remember something. You have me, Amaryliss and Reginald now. You don't have to do things alone anymore," he whispers in my ear.

His words hit me hard. For as long as I can remember, I've been trying to keep things together for mom and myself. I became independent at a young age, so mom wouldn't have to worry and always did things myself. With mom gone, I thought I would be truly alone, but now I am beginning to understand. My father didn't just leave me a manor, he left me a family that will help me through this new stage in my life. Well, undead life.

"I guess this is the end of my human life, huh?" I ask as I rest my head against his shoulder.

His hand raises to my chin, and he lifts my head to meet his eyes. Darren's gentle gaze makes my heart flutter, and my eyes are transfixed on his fangs. Soon I will have a set too and feed on the blood on the innocence or something like that.

"It's not the end, Elizabeth. No. It's only the beginning."

He caresses my cheek and pulls my face closer, carefully placing his lips on mine. He kisses me tenderly, and any doubts in mind slowly start to slip away.

THE END.

ABOUT THE AUTHOR

I was born and raised in Reading, Pennsylvania, before settling down in Ephrata, Pennsylvania. Reading and writing have been a lifelong interest that eventually became my life. When I'm not writing, im either eating sushi watching horror movies or catching up on my favorite Animes. Blood & Butlers is my debut novel with many more to come.

Follow me on social media!

Facebook: @AuthorSJFrey
Instagram: @Author_sjfrey
Twitter: @Author_SJF
Website: authorsjfrey1.wixsite.com/authorpage

BLOOD & BETRAYAL

COMING SOON!

Made in the USA
Middletown, DE
02 January 2020